MURDER

ON THE OLD BOG ROAD

Gripping Irish crime fiction

DAVID PEARSON

THE
BOOK
FOLKS

Paperback edition published by

The Book Folks

London, 2018

© David Pearson

ISBN 978-1-9807-0515-4

www.thebookfolks.com

For Barbara, without whose support this book would not have been possible.

Chapter One

Ciara O'Sullivan left the shop in Galway just as soon as it closed its doors at six o'clock. It was a foul night, with the westerly wind driving the rain down onto the slick roads and footpaths, and Ciara wasn't looking forward to the drive out to Clifden. But she had promised to visit her ailing mother, as she did every week, out in the old family home on the main street in the west of Ireland town.

Ciara was assistant manager at the large, brightly lit emporium called 'About the House' on Galway's Shop Street. As the name suggested, the shop sold all manner of household items, from a simple kitchen utensil right up to a full suite of furniture, or a bed, and even stocked a few rugs and carpets. Ciara had got the job there soon after graduating from University College Galway where she had studied retail management, and she enjoyed it immensely.

Ciara was a good-looking girl, standing straight at five foot nine inches tall, with a trim figure, and a mane of shiny auburn hair that fell half way down her back. She

3

had inherited her mother's high cheekbones, and with her large dark brown eyes and full mouth, she was very striking, and was often admired by the men who visited the shop. Some would say she was the epitome of an Irish *cailín*.

She was glad she had parked the car nearby in Hynes' Yard car park. This was no night for umbrellas, so she donned a sturdy tweed cap, pulled her raincoat tightly around her and with her head down, she wound her way through the narrow streets to the sanctuary of the car park where her little Ford Fiesta was waiting, out of the weather.

Ciara had been very pleased to have passed her driving test first time the previous year, as this meant she could visit her mother regularly once a week to see that she was eating well, and had a good supply of medication, and that her house in Clifden was warm and dry on these winter nights. It had been a bit of a struggle to save up for the little Ford, and she didn't fancy the idea of buying it on credit, but she had managed all the same, and loved the little car which seemed to be virtually indestructible, no matter what the occasion.

The traffic in the city was heavy, and the incessant rain made progress slow. Despite the heater in the car being on full, the windows kept steaming up, and Ciara had to wipe them constantly to maintain a modicum of visibility. It was almost twenty to seven by the time she got free of the traffic and started out on the N59 heading for Moycullen and Oughterard. Her mother had asked her to stop in to Roundstone on the way, where the woman who ran the Lake Guest House, now empty of tourists at this time of year, had been making a new set of curtains for

Mrs. O'Sullivan's spare bedroom, the old ones having literally fallen to pieces from old age some time ago. The woman who ran the guest house turned her hand to sewing as soon as the tourist season came to an end, to make some pin money for the winter months, and she was known to be an excellent seamstress.

When Ciara got past Oughterard, the conditions deteriorated even further. The rain pelted down so that Ciara's windscreen wipers could barely keep the window clear, and she had to slow down to hold the car on the correct side of the road, fighting the buffeting wind all the way. But west of Ireland people were used to these conditions, so she pressed on regardless.

At Roundstone she managed to resist the insistence of the guest house owner to stop and have a cup of tea and some freshly made scones, saying that her mother would be expecting her and would be worried given the night that was in it. She took the curtains, which had been carefully sealed into two plastic bags, and resumed her journey out west along the old bog road.

As Ciara emerged from the scant shelter of the hills approaching Ballyconneely, the weather got even worse. The rain was being driven horizontally off the sea, and now mixed with salt water, was even harder to clear from the windscreen. Ciara slowed to a crawl and edged her way along with her headlights on full beam. She was thankful that on such a night, there was no other traffic about.

As she approached the bridge by the beach, she saw that several large stones had been dislodged, and were strewn across the road. She brought her car to a halt, and realised that she would need to get out and move the rocks in order to continue safely. She cursed silently under her breath, and opened the driver's door which was nearly taken off its hinges by the force of the wind. Outside the car, the strong wind was blowing a mixture of sea spray, mist and turf smoke from the cottages between the road and the sea, and she pulled her jacket tightly around her. She moved the obstructing stones away to the side using both her hands and feet, and as she finished with one large stone, placing it in the ditch on the left-hand side of the road, she spotted a large piece of what looked like red fabric in the gully itself.

She went over to where the cloth was sticking out, and as she approached, she saw that there was a lot more of it than she had first noticed. When she was standing over the ditch, she looked down and saw that it was in fact a red coat, and it was wrapped around a young woman, who was lying, lifeless, partly submerged in the bog water. She recoiled from the horror of the scene. Ignoring the fact that she was getting soaked to the skin, Ciara stood there for several minutes, her hand held to her mouth, and tears trickling from her big brown eyes. "God, what will I do?" she asked herself.

She went back to the car, and took out her mobile phone, but of course there was no signal. The phone was of no use to her.

"I'd better get help," she thought, and decided to drive on into Clifden where she would be able to report it to the local Garda. They'd know what to do.

* * *

Ciara pulled up outside the Garda station in Clifden and got out of the car. The rain had eased off just a little, but it would be back soon with increased ferocity, of that she had no doubt. Although there was a light on outside the station, the door was locked, and it looked as if there was no one inside. Ciara knocked loudly on the door all the same. The station should still be manned at this hour.

As she stood there, a man came along the footpath, huddled against the weather and saw Ciara banging on the door.

"Is that you, Ciara?" he shouted against the wind. "Sure it is. Are you looking for the sergeant?" he said, answering his own question and asking another.

"Oh hi, Séamus, yes, but he doesn't seem to be here."

"Ah sure, don't ye know he'll be down at Cusheen's having a pint before he heads home. He's always there at this time," the man said.

"Ah you're right of course, I had forgotten his routine. I'll head down there now."

"Are ye OK, Ciara, you look a bit pale?" Seamus enquired.

"Sure, I'm grand Séamus, don't worry. I'd best be off to see himself. Good night."

Chapter Two

Sergeant Séan Mulholland took a long draw on his third pint of Guinness that evening. He sat alone at a table beside the warm turf fire in Cusheen's Bar right in the centre of Clifden. He had almost finished reading the paper from cover to cover and was thinking he'd have just one more pint before going back out in the weather and on home.

Mulholland was one of the eleven members of the force attached to Clifden and was officially known as the Member in Charge. Since the closure of tens of rural Garda stations in 2011, following the financial meltdown in Ireland, Clifden now covered most of West Galway from Recess out to beyond Letterfrack, where Westport Garda took over. Roundstone was still officially open, but it was a one-man station, and the Garda there spent most of his time assigned to Clifden in any case, especially if there was something serious going down. Clifden was supposed to have two Garda vehicles, but one of these had crashed, so the individual Gardaí used their own cars on an allowance basis, and had blue lights and sirens fitted to help them in their work.

Mulholland was fifty-eight years old and could have retired on full pension, but being a bachelor and living on his own, he enjoyed the camaraderie that membership of the force afforded him, and the small amount of status that his years of service and his rank bestowed upon him. He was well known in the district, and if he wasn't exactly adored by everyone, he was well respected.

The lifestyle suited him well enough. Clifden had very little crime, and his time was mostly taken up with the renewal of shotgun licenses for the local farmers who shot rabbit out on the various headlands in the area. He had some other light administrative duties too that kept him busy at the station, completing monthly returns for Galway and managing the rosters for the other Gardaí at the station. Occasionally there had been some break-ins at some of the holiday cottages up along the Sky Road, or out towards Ballyconneely, but the thieves soon tired of that, as these places yielded little of value, and their chances of being caught were fairly high – there essentially being just three routes out of the town.

The Garda station in Clifden was supposed to stay open from eight am to eight pm each day, but Mulholland usually shut up shop at around six thirty, especially in winter when there was nothing happening.

"Sure, they know where to find me if they need me," he would say, referring to his nightly routine of going to Cusheen's for three or four pints and a quiet read of the paper before heading home out the Sky Road to his small, rather damp and very drab cottage.

Cusheen's was one of Clifden's oldest and most traditional pubs. Unlike others in the town it had been spared the makeover that ran rampant through almost all the other pubs during the Celtic Tiger years. It was dark, simple, with a stone flagged floor, a decent bar, and a good array of comfortable chairs and small tables scattered around, and of course the obligatory turf fire which was most welcome on a night such as this.

* * *

Crashing through the double doors of the bar, Ciara spotted the sergeant seated at a table near the fire reading the paper.

"Sergeant, I need to talk to you. It's urgent," she said, the words spilling out as she struggled to catch her breath.

"Christ, Ciara, it's yourself. You look drowned. Sit down there a minute. Can I get you a drink?"

"No, I'll not sit. You need to come with me now. See, there's a body out the road," she said, regaining a modicum of composure.

"A body, is it. What is it? A sheep or a dog, or maybe a donkey," he said smiling.

"No, Sergeant, it's a woman. She's lying in the ditch in a red coat out by Ballyconneely. I think she's dead," she said.

"Good God, why didn't you say so. Let's go and see what all this is about then," said Mulholland rising from the table and draining the last of his pint.

"You'd better drive, and we'll go in your car," he said.

The two sat in silence as Ciara drove the little Ford back out the old bog road towards Ballyconneely. The rain had stopped for the time being, and the moon shone through the patchy cloud from time to time casting an eerie glow on the landscape.

As they approached the bridge with its dry-stone walls Ciara spoke up. "It's just here, Sergeant. She's in the ditch down by the bridge. You can see a bit of her red coat."

The car came to a halt and they got out, the sergeant putting on his peaked cap, as if that would in some way make his presence more official. Mulholland shone his torch up and down the ditch until the beam landed on the pale blue face of the young woman half covered with her lank dark brown hair.

"Good God," he said out loud as he clambered down awkwardly to feel the woman's neck for a pulse, and was not surprised to find that there was none.

"She's dead all right," he proclaimed, "God this is awful. I'll call Jim Dolan on the radio. I'll get him to call Galway and get an ambulance and an inspector out, and then come on out here himself in the squad car. We need to preserve the scene," Mulholland said, struggling back onto the side of the road, his training clearly cutting in, although he had never had to deal with anything like this before.

* * *

An hour later and they could see the blue flashing lights reflected in the low mist long before the vehicles came into sight. Garda Dolan had arrived twenty minutes earlier and slewed the ten-year-old white Mondeo across the road with its own blue lights winking in the gloom. He had attempted to put up blue and white tape around the scene, but the wind took most of it, with just a few well anchored strands fluttering about.

The convoy of Galway vehicles arrived. In front, the newer Garda Hyundai estate car carried Inspector Mick Hays, two uniformed Gardaí and the pathologist from Galway Regional Hospital. Next came a Garda Toyota four by four with three scene of crime technicians along with a generator, three flood lights and an inflatable plastic tent. Bringing up the rear was an emergency ambulance with two paramedics and an array of medical kit, almost certainly of little use on this occasion.

Hays was first out of the vehicles and as he walked over to where Mulholland and Ciara were standing said, "Hello Séan. Haven't seen you for a while. What have you got here for me then?"

"How are ya, Mick? Yes, it's been a while. Ciara here," he said, nodding to the girl who was standing off giving the two policemen some space, "Ciara here says she was on her way to Clifden when she came across a woman lying in the ditch." Mulholland went on to outline the events leading to the call to the Regional Crime Centre in Galway where Hays was based.

Mick Hays turned to Ciara, "Miss O'Sullivan, can you tell me what you were doing out along this road at nine-thirty at night?"

"I was on my way to Clifden to see my mother. She's not well, and I like to visit her every week if I can. She lives alone in the main street," Ciara explained.

"And where do you live yourself?" Hays enquired.

"I have a place in Galway. I work there as a retail manageress, and I have my own flat."

"Did you see any other vehicle at all on the road, or anyone about?" Hays asked.

"No, I saw nothing and no one since I left Roundstone till I came to this very spot."

"What made you stop?"

"I had to swerve out to avoid some rocks that had come down from the side of the bridge, and then I saw her red coat in the headlights, so I stopped to take a look," she said.

"Right so. Can you wait here till we get a few details, and we'll need to get a statement from you tomorrow, but you can get on into Clifden shortly. As a matter of interest, why did you come this way? Would the main road not have been quicker?"

"I had to collect some curtains for my mother at the Lake Guest House in Roundstone. She's been waiting on them," Ciara said.

"Fair enough, we'll leave it be for now. Just give your details to Garda Dolan, then be on your way."

* * *

Dr Julian Dodd was not a native of Galway but had taken the post of pathologist at the regional hospital to avoid having to emigrate. It had worked out well, and he was now firmly established in the post and highly regarded by his colleagues for his thoroughness and intuition.

Now in his mid-fifties, he was a man of some five foot ten inches tall with a mop of curly hair that would have been unruly if he did not have it cut regularly. He had been at a dinner with friends when he got the call to come out to Connemara, so he looked a bit out of place in a smart Ralph Lauren Polo button down shirt, tweed jacket and slacks. His shiny black shoes were already muddy and stained from the bog water, but Dodd ignored this as he went about his job with what was approaching enthusiasm.

The white inflatable tent that they had tried to position over the body had been taken by the wind, so the good doctor and the paramedics were hunched over the ditch where the woman lay when Hays approached.

"Well, Doc, what are your first thoughts?" Hays asked.

"Very few for now, Inspector. She's definitely deceased, that's for sure, but beyond that, there's not a lot to say as yet," he replied rather formally, as was his style.

"Any idea how long?" Hays persisted.

"Probably between three and five hours ago, but immersion in the water hasn't made it easy to be certain."

"Did she drown?"

"I can't tell you till I get her back to Galway and open her up, but intuitively I'd say no. There's no ditch water in her mouth or nostrils. But I can tell you one thing, she's taken a severe blow to the back of the skull."

"I see. Any idea what the weapon might have been, or could she just have fallen against the stones?"

"I doubt that. It could have been a rock, or a flat instrument of some kind – perhaps a spade. But I'll be able to tell you more tomorrow when I've had a good look."

"No chance she was run over?" Hays asked.

"I don't think so, no. In fact, I'd say definitely not. If I had to guess, I'd say she was whacked from behind with something and then fell or was pushed down into the ditch. She was probably dead before she hit the water. Get your boys to look for a squarish stone that you could hold in your hand that's been chucked away a bit. You might find the murder weapon close by, but don't quote me. Anyway, that's your job, not mine."

14

"Great. A loose rock around here – now where would you find one of those? Can we move her yet?"

"Yes, you can get her into the ambulance now."

Hays gave the go ahead for the woman's body to be put in the ambulance but asked one of the scene of crime officers to search her pockets for any identification before she was taken away.

Hays returned to where Sergeant Mulholland was talking to the two uniformed Gardaí that had come out from Galway.

"Séan, can you leave Dolan here for the night on point? Our team will be back in the morning to do a fingertip search of the site. I want to get back to Galway and inform the superintendent. What do you know about this Ciara O'Sullivan?"

"Oh, she's a grand lass. They are a good family, never in any trouble. Her father died about five years ago, and her mother is elderly and a bit poorly. She lives in the town, and the girl comes out to see her every week. She has a good job in the city."

"Hmm, OK, well we will get a detailed statement from her tomorrow and take her fingerprints too and a DNA swab – 'for the purpose of elimination', as we say."

"Surely you don't suspect her, Mick? She's just a slip of a lass," Mulholland said.

"She's probably in the clear, but she was the first to find the body, and you know what they say, so let's not take any chances Séan," Hays said.

As Hays was talking to the forensic team, an old white van came along the road from the direction of Roundstone, and pulled up in front of Jim Dolan's squad car. A man got out and walked over to where Séan Mulholland was leaning against the car.

"Good evening, Sergeant, what's the story?" he asked.

"Oh, hello Gerry. God it's awful. We're after finding a girl here down in the ditch, and on such a night. It's terrible."

"Is she OK?" Gerry Maguire asked, looking concerned.

"No, she's not OK, Gerry. She's dead."

"Jesus, merciful hour. What in God's name happened to her?"

"I can't say any more for now, Gerry. What has you out at this time anyway?"

"I'm just on my way back from a job in Roundstone, Sergeant. Mary will be wondering where I've got to," Maguire replied.

"And did you see anyone else on the road at all?" the sergeant enquired.

"No, not a soul. Sure, who would be out on a night like this? But listen, I better be on my way. If I can be of any help, or if you need to get a cuppa tea or anything, come on down to the house. We'll be there, and it's no trouble."

"Fair enough, Gerry, that's good of you, but I better stay on my toes here, what with the big brass out from Galway, if you know what I mean," the sergeant responded, and with that, Gerry Maguire got back into his van and navigated around the parked cars and left the scene.

Chapter Three

Detective Sergeant Maureen Lyons was already at her desk when Hays arrived on Wednesday morning. Lyons was a small thirty-two-year-old brunette with a trim figure and a cute face. She had large brown eyes, and her hair was down to her shoulders, though she almost always wore it in a ponytail at work.

Maureen Lyons had wanted to join the force since she was sixteen years old. Her father had been a sergeant based in Loughrea, but had spent much of his service in and around the border area during the troubles of the 1970s and early 80s. Even at a young age, Maureen was fascinated by the stories he would tell of his investigation into various crimes, and how the detectives had worked a range of clues to finally bring wrong-doers to justice. She had enrolled in the Garda Síochana in her final year at school and headed off to the training college in Templemore in the autumn of the year that she had completed her secondary education.

Lyons had earned her stripes early in her career by single-handedly foiling an armed raid on the Permanent TSB Bank in Galway four years earlier. She had been on the beat around Eyre Square and was just passing the bank when an armed raider in a balaclava had burst out the door carrying a supermarket bag full of cash in one hand and a sawn-off shotgun in the other. Lyons had simply stuck out her foot tripping the thief who fell flat on his face, unable to break his fall due to his hands being full. Gun and money went flying. The robber broke his nose and was stunned, bleeding profusely, so Maureen took the opportunity to handcuff him, and of course arrest him then and there. Talk about being in the right place at the right time.

The media, and in fairness the Garda publicity teams, had milked the story mercilessly. "Pocket Rocket Bean Garda foils armed raid" declared the headlines in the Connaught Tribune. In the interviews that followed on Radio, TV and for the print media, Maureen had been very understated and modest about her new-found celebrity status.

"Sure, I was just doing my job," she would say shyly, "any other member of the force would have done the same," she had said with a twinkle in her big brown eyes.

After a decent interval following her heroics when the media circus had moved on, she was made up to sergeant and invited to join the detective unit, a role that she eagerly accepted. In the two years since she started working for Mick Hays she had proved her worth over and over. Her sharp instincts and logical mental processes had helped solve many tricky cases, and she was generally well regarded in the unit.

"Morning Maureen. I suppose you heard about the drama last night out Clifden way. Had me up half the bloody night," Hays grumbled.

"Yes, Boss. I've been reading the notes. Do we have any idea who the poor woman is yet?"

"Not a clue. No identification, no handbag, no phone, nada," said Hays.

"We need to set up an incident room straight away. Can you grab a room and get a whiteboard and a few computers, phones and stuff set up? And get Flynn and O'Connor in, we'll have a briefing in an hour."

"The Super is going nuts. He knows when the press gets hold of it they'll go to town. You can just see it now, 'Wild night of murder on the Wild Atlantic Way,'" he mimicked, using his hands to draw an imaginary headline.

"Still, maybe it's not all bad. You know what they say about publicity, and there are enough gawkers around to make the scene a tourist attraction in its own right," she said.

At nine-thirty in the Corrib Room, Mick Hays called the briefing to order. He had Maureen Lyons, a Detective Garda Eamon Flynn and a uniformed Garda John O'Connor assigned immediately to the case and he knew he could get more resources if he needed them as the investigation moved forward.

Hays outlined the events of the previous night in as much detail as he could for the team. A single ten by four photo of the dead girl taken from where she lay in the ditch had been pinned to the whiteboard, with a large red question mark beside it. The name Ciara O'Sullivan also appeared on the board, but no photo. And that was it.

"Our priority is to identify the victim. We need that before we can start looking for a motive or an opportunity," Hays said.

"The post mortem is at ten-thirty. I'll need you with me, Maureen, the victim is female, so you can give us the female perspective on things."

Maureen bristled slightly at the near sexist remark, but let it go. She knew Mick Hays wasn't biased against women either in or out of the force. He was just winding her up ever so slightly.

"John, I want you on the computers all day. We need background on the girl that found the body for starters. When she comes in this evening to make a statement, we'll get more. Then do the usual missing persons trawl. Include Northern Ireland as well," Hays instructed.

He then turned his attention to Detective Flynn. "Can you get over to forensics? I want to know the moment they find anything of interest out at the scene. Stay close for the day and call me with anything that comes up."

"Well OK, Boss, but they're only just getting started, it could be a while before they have anything."

"That's why I'm sending you over there, Eamon, to give them a kick up the arse."

Mick Hays didn't like post mortems much. The smell, the apparent disregard for the dignity of a body that a couple of days ago had been a vibrant, living being bothered him too. And then there was the slightly superior air of the pathologist with a "what would you know" attitude to deal with. Dodd was quite good at being superior in his own surroundings while trying to impress his obvious ability on the two or three trainees that invariably attended these morbid affairs. But Hays had to admit that he was damn good at his job too. He had helped to untangle many a knotty problem for the detective over the years they had worked together.

The girl was laid out on the slab, with a block under her head, facing upwards as if staring blankly at the ceiling.

"Well, Doc, what have you got for us then?" Hays asked.

"Very little so far. As I said last night, she appears to have died from a blow to the back of her head. Time of death between five and nine yesterday. She died where she was found. The blow was a severe one. From the angle and the severity of it I'd say she was struck by a man, or maybe a tall strong woman, wielding a stone or a rock. We found tiny slivers of feldspar in the wound, so that rules out a spade. It wasn't frenzied, there was just one, single fatal blow, but he intended to kill her, you don't whack someone that hard to get their attention."

"Anything to identify her?" Hays asked.

"Precious little, I'm afraid. Her teeth have never been filled, so there won't be any dental records. But there are one or two indicators that may be helpful," Dodd said.

"She's younger than we thought. Twenty-three or four, six at most. The skeletal development and teeth are that of an early to mid-twenties female."

"Was she pregnant?" Lyons asked.

"Good question, detective. No, she wasn't or isn't, but she has had an abortion some time ago. Nice job too, not the usual knife and fork job. Would have been expensive."

"How long ago?" Lyons asked.

"More than a year is all I can say, and no more than five years ago, so sometime between the ages of say seventeen to twenty-two," he said.

"Oh, and we found this," Dodd said, scooping up a small plastic bag from the bench and holding it out in front of him at arm's length like a small trophy.

"It was on the arm folded beneath her in the ditch, so we didn't spot it last night," he said.

Lyons took the bag and examined the contents. It contained a gold bangle about a centimetre wide with a spring clasp and a tiny safety chain.

"You can take it out, there are no prints on it," the doctor said.

Lyons removed the bangle from the bag and examined it closely.

"It's foreign," she said. "It has the number 916 stamped inside which means it's twenty-two carat gold, but not from round here. I think that's a European stamp," she added.

"Anything from her clothes that might help us to identify her?" Hays asked.

"Nothing. All the labels have been cut off and I've looked really thoroughly. Sometimes a maker will leave a label internally somewhere, like inside a lining or something, but there's absolutely nothing. All I can say is that her clothes are generally of good quality, that's about it," the doctor remarked.

"I don't suppose we'd be lucky enough to find she was full of semen?" Hays asked.

Lyons gave him a scornful glance.

"Nope. Not a drop. There has been recent sexual activity, but fully protected, I'm afraid. Vaginal only before you ask," Dodd said.

"OK, Doc. We're heading back to the station now. Let one of us know if you find anything else. We need to be able to identify this girl as soon as possible," Hays said.

Chapter Four

Hays and Lyons arrived back at the station at around one-thirty having eaten a hasty sandwich in the pub across the road. Hays called the team together and updated them on the initial results from the post mortem. He then asked John O'Connor for any information that he had managed to dig up during their absence.

"Nothing much to report," he said. "The girl that found the body seems to be as clean as a whistle – not even a speeding ticket or a parking fine. Yer man Maguire that turned up while you were there has a bit of previous, but only small stuff, no tax and insurance about five years ago, that sort of thing. Oh, and a bit of hijinks when he was younger. He slapped a Garda outside a pub, but he got off with a fine. We have his prints and stuff on file though.

"Then I went onto Pulse to look for missing person reports. Nothing there either. There was only one report that fits the timeframe and that's for an eighty-six-year-old male who wandered off from his care home in Port Laoise."

"Good work, John, thanks, even if you came up with zilch," Hays grunted.

"We really need to find out who this girl is. John, can you get a few hundred hand-bills made up with her picture – cheer it up a bit, try to make her look a little less dead. Get all the uniformed Gardaí to hand them out around the town, put them up in shops, bars – you know the drill, 'Have you seen this woman? Gardaí are urgently seeking information…' that sort of thing."

"Sure, I'll get onto it right away," O'Connor responded and left the room.

Turning to Eamon Flynn, Hays said, "Eamon, I want you to take this bangle down to a jeweller. Hartmans would be a good bet. See if they can tell you where it's from, or anything else about it. They might even have sold it, though I doubt if we'd be that lucky. Ask roughly how much it's worth, and what sort of age it has."

"Maureen, you're for the old bog road again I'm afraid. Get back out there and see if the search team has found anything. And have a nosey around too. Kick up some dust, turn over a few stones. You can take a uniformed Garda with you and let him out in Roundstone to poke around a bit. Someone knows something. She didn't fall from the sky, that's for sure," Hays said.

"Oh, and while you're there, shake up the local Garda a bit too. Tell Mulholland the Super is talking about calling out to see him. It's all a bit laid back out in Clifden for my liking," Hays said.

"And while I'm enjoying the scenery out in Ballyconneely, what are you going to do?" Maureen asked.

She was peeved at having to drive all the way out to Clifden at this time of day just to spend a few hours making herself unpopular and then driving back, and she was concerned that Hays was sidelining her from the investigation.

Hays ignored the irony and replied, "I'm heading on over to Ciara O'Sullivan's shop. I want to get a statement from her today. She might have remembered something important overnight."

Lyons gave him a filthy look. This Ciara O'Sullivan was one good looking woman.

"OK that's it for now, off you go. We'll meet back here at six or half past – all except the tourists," he said, giving Lyons a harsh stare, "Maureen, will you phone in at six-thirty with any update?" Hays asked.

"Yes Boss, if I can get a signal," she replied, still smarting from the task that she had been given.

* * *

Hartmans is one of the largest and longest established jewellers in Galway, and they rightly pride themselves on the quality of their wares, and a very thorough knowledge of their trade. Eamon Flynn knew the shop, but not well, and not from the inside at all. The glittering baubles that festooned the brightly lit windows, the rows of watches with names such as Rolex, Raymond Weil, Rotary, Longines were well out of reach for a humble Garda. Even as he entered the premises, the aura of expensive merchandise, the gleam of the bright lights and the slightly scented air almost took his breath away.

No sooner had he stepped up to the counter when a truly beautiful girl with perfect make-up and long shiny blonde hair immaculately groomed approached him.

"Good afternoon, sir, how can I help you?" she said in perfect English with no hint of an accent of any kind.

Flynn produced his warrant card, introducing himself to the girl whose brightly polished gold name badge identified her as Monika, with a "k".

Flynn produced the gold bangle, still in its plastic evidence bag and offered it to the girl.

"We were wondering if you could tell us anything about this item?" he asked. "It's connected to an investigation that I'm working on," he added.

Monika took the bangle out of its wrapping and placed it on a small piece of green velvet on the counter. She turned it over a few times. "Well I'm fairly sure it's not one of ours. Do you mind if I call Charles to have a look at it?" she asked.

"Thanks, that would be great," Flynn replied, enjoying the view of Monika's rear as she walked into the back of the shop to fetch Charles.

Charles was tall, slim and very elegant, dressed in a sharp navy pinstripe suit with an immaculate starched white shirt and maroon tie. He sported a magnificent pair of gold cufflinks and a very expensive watch.

"The detective wants to know if we can tell him anything about this bangle," Monika said, pointing to the gold bracelet sitting on the green velvet cloth.

Charles picked it up and slowly rotated it on both axes, examining it closely, but saying nothing.

He reached into his jacket pocket and took out his jeweller's loupe, holding it to his right eye as he scrutinized the bangle, focusing on the area around the clasp and safety chain.

"Yes, well this is interesting," he said at last removing the loupe. "It's definitely not Irish. It's very good quality, not the usual mass-produced tat. Judging by the way the clasp is made I'd say it's almost certainly German. It's made from very high-quality gold. It's twenty-two carat – you can tell that from the 916 stamp, and the safety chain is probably eighteen carat with a little less gold for greater strength. It's a fine piece. May I ask where you came across it, detective?" Charles asked.

"I can't say, I'm afraid, it's part of an ongoing investigation. How much would you say it's worth?" Flynn enquired.

"In the order of seven to eight hundred euro when new I should say. Whoever owns it will miss it."

"Any idea how old it might be?"

"Not old, and not worn everyday either. I'd say it was made within the last five years or so. The design is quite contemporary," Charles said.

"Well thank you both very much for your help," Flynn said, picking up the bangle and putting it back into the evidence bag. As he turned to leave the shop he stole a final glance at Monika who was smiling sweetly at him.

* * *

Hays strolled from the Garda Station on Mill Street to the centre of town, and readily found About The House brightly lit and full of fashionable homewares on Shop Street. He was no sooner inside the door than he was approached by an assistant who asked how she could help him. He asked to see Miss O'Sullivan and was ushered to a counter with a flask of tea and coffee, milk and sugar, and instructed to help himself while the girl went off to find Ciara.

A few moments later, Ciara appeared, looking a lot better than she had at the side of the road the previous evening. She smiled warmly at Hays and asked if he would like to talk in her office, which was on the second floor at the back of the display area.

Ciara O'Sullivan's office was small, but perfectly formed with contemporary office furniture, and an enormous lamp that was anchored in the corner, but rose on a long semi-circular arc, and was finished in a bowl like shade with one of those new-fangled bulbs that doesn't give out much light but looks retro. Hays was ushered into a comfortable office chair opposite Ciara's cherrywood desk.

"How can I help you today?" she asked, still smiling warmly at the inspector.

"Oh, it's just routine really. We need to get a formal account of what happened last night when you were on your way out to see your mother. How is she by the way, I understand she has been a bit poorly?"

"She's not very well, Inspector, but she's not in any pain, and she potters around the house most days, and the neighbours are very kind to her. Winter is hard on old people though, don't you think?"

"Yes, yes, it is. Well, if you could just go through the events of the night again, I'll write down what you say, and then I'll ask you to sign it if that's OK?"

Ciara recounted the story much as she had told it the previous night at the roadside, and Hays copied down her words as succinctly as he could. When she was finished, he drew a line through the remaining free space on the page and turned it around for her to sign.

"What will happen to this?" she asked, looking straight at the inspector.

"How do you mean?"

"Well, will I be needed to give evidence or something? I haven't been involved with the police before, I don't know the drill."

"Oh, I see. Well it's possible, depending on the way the case goes, but we're a long way from that at this point. I shouldn't worry about it if I were you, and in any case, you've given a statement. Is there anything at all, no matter how small, that you have remembered since last night? It must have been a terrible shock for you," Hays re-assured her.

"Yes, it was. I didn't sleep very well, I can tell you."

"That will pass, trust me. Well, if there's nothing more, I'd better be off."

When Hays got up to leave, Ciara came round the desk and they both arrived at the office door at the same time. Hays couldn't be sure, but he definitely felt her push gently up against him, and her scent filled his nostrils as they both reached for the door handle together. Ciara made no move to step back, and there was no embarrassment as he stood back to let her out in front of him.

"Great shop you have here. You have it really nicely done out. Where did you learn your trade?" Hays asked as they made their way back through the store towards the entrance.

"I did retail management in UCG. It was a terrific course, and I had six months in Liberty's in London for work experience, so I stole a few of their ideas I'm afraid."

"Well, it seems to be working. Thanks for your time," and he shook hands with her at the shop door and left.

* * *

The team met back in the incident room at six thirty, all except Maureen Lyons who would probably still be fifty miles away, in or near Clifden.

"Right," Hays said, calling the meeting to order, "let's see what we have so far."

"What do we know about the deceased? Apart from the obvious, her age and appearance, we know she was dressed in good quality clothing, and she had that expensive gold bangle on her arm. She has had an abortion at some stage, but not a backstreet job, and she has been sexually active with a man, so we know that at least one person has been close to her in the recent past, as well as the murderer of course – could be the same person, we don't know for now. Dodd says her hair was well groomed by a hairdresser, and what was left of her make-up was expensive stuff too. So, this girl was not a pauper. John, any news on the hand-bills?" Hays asked.

"They've been printed up and the lads are out now putting them up around the place. I've sent some out to Sergeant Mulholland as well, so he can get them circulated in Clifden, Roundstone, Ballyconneely and so on," the young Garda reported.

"Good stuff. Let's hope we get a response."

"What about the bangle, Eamon?"

Flynn recounted the visit to the Hartmans, leaving out his views on the lovely Monika.

"So, the girl might possibly be foreign then, although let's not get ahead of ourselves just yet on that one," Hays said.

They were interrupted by the phone ringing, and Hays walked over to the desk and picked it up. It was Lyons calling from the wilderness. Hays put the phone on speaker and said, "Go ahead, Maureen, we're all ears."

"Well you needn't bother on my account," Lyons said crossly, "there's bugger all to report from here. No forensics at all, not even a decent tyre track. Just a tiny scratch on one of the stones dislodged from the bridge, but no paint or plastic on it. A complete waste of time. Tell me you have better news there," she said.

"Not a lot here either, Maureen. We have leaflets with the girl's photo being circulated. Oh, and Eamon reckons the bangle she was wearing is probably German, so she may be foreign, which accounts for the fact that there's no missing person's report."

"What about the girl? Anything more from Dodd?" asked Lyons.

"Not much. She ate her last meal of fish and salad at about three pm. She had a couple of glasses of white wine with the meal. There are no tattoos, no external scars or birth marks, nothing that could help identify her," Hays said.

"OK, well I'm leaving here now. The techies have packed up. I passed on your good wishes to Sergeant Mulholland. I take it you don't need me any more tonight, Boss?"

"No that's fine. We'll meet at eight-thirty tomorrow to plan the day. Thanks Maureen."

Lyons clicked off the phone without saying goodbye and was gone.

* * *

On the way back to the city in her car, Lyons spent the journey trying to figure out exactly where she stood with Mick Hays. They got on well most of the time, but she didn't know how much he was really willing to trust her with the more challenging aspects of an investigation. Her father had told her that it took a long time to work up a reliable reputation in An Garda Síochana, and while she never really questioned her own ability, she didn't have any idea what the rest of the team really thought of her.

When she eventually got home, she had talked herself into rather a glum mood. It didn't last long though. Relaxing in her cosy apartment, she determined that she would show Hays, and the rest of the team, just how competent she could be. "Don't let the bastards grind you down" as her father told her regularly.

Chapter Five

Wednesday, 11:00 am

The two German hikers had breakfasted well at Eldon's Hotel in Roundstone where they had stayed the previous night. They had planned their day with as much precision as the weather and their mood would permit. It was a bright cool blustery day in Roundstone, ideal for their planned exploration of Inishnee, an untamed island just off the coast, connected to the village by a rickety bridge, and with just a few old cottages dotted around the place. They had then planned to hike into Clifden out along the old bog road.

Their guide book told them that it was twenty-two kilometres from Roundstone to Clifden, so by leaving Roundstone at eleven-thirty they could hope to reach Clifden by five pm just as darkness was falling.

They had taken a packed lunch from the hotel as they were told there was no shop or hostelry available until they reached Ballyconneely itself by which time they would be famished. The walk was pleasant. They stopped to admire the view looking down over Dog's Bay with its two horse-shoe shaped beaches of white sand glistening in the morning light. They could see a few sheep grazing on the short grass out on the headland and the old abandoned caravan site down by the sea. They stopped again further on at Murvey and several of the other beauty spots along the road. The weather was holding up well, with fluffy cotton wool clouds scurrying across in front of the weak winter sun. After two hours of walking, as they approached Murlach, just before the road heads inland they decided to stop for lunch.

There was a small lay-by at the side of the road with some large flat rocks that would do nicely for seating and a makeshift table, although it was a bit overgrown with brambles. The ground rose up steeply behind the lay-by, so that they were sheltered from the stiffening breeze. They managed to find a clear space to sit, and spread out the sandwiches, cakes and cold drinks that the hotel had provided for them.

No sooner had they started their meal when they heard a faint beeping sound coming from the bushy undergrowth. They looked around but could see nothing, but there it was again, a clear, if faint, electronic 'beep beep' coming from nearby.

The man was curious by nature, so he took his walking pole and started poking around in the undergrowth near to where he felt the noise was coming from. There it was again. A distinctive 'beep beep', a little louder now as he had cleared some of the covering foliage. His girlfriend asked him to stop being so nosey and come back and finish his lunch. But he persisted, and as he knocked back the tangled shrubs and prickly brambles with the stick, he soon found the source of the noise. Lying partly covered by the leaves of a fern, the pale green shape of a Nokia mobile phone was revealed. He reached in, being careful not to snag his hand on the thorns, and gently lifted the little phone out.

'Low Battery' was displayed on the small monochrome LCD screen, and just to make the point, the phone emitted another two rather anaemic beeps.

"Look. I told you there was something. It's a small Nokia that's running out of battery. We must hand it in when we get to Clifden. Perhaps someone is needing it."

They finished their meal and tidied away the wrappings and empty drinks cans carefully, and then walked on through the afternoon, passing the golden strand at Ballyconneely. The stiff breeze had started to whip up the sea. They walked on into Clifden, arriving very much on time at just after five o'clock as darkness was falling. They were booked into the Atlantic Coast Hotel which they found easily, electing to shower and have an early meal before going to find the police station to hand in the phone.

When they had finished their meal, they enquired about the location of the local police station and were told by the hotel receptionist how to get there. When they had noted this down, the receptionist added, "but it's all locked up now for the night. But if you need something, the sergeant will be in Cusheen's Bar just over the road. He's always there till eight or nine," she explained.

They looked at each other with some curiosity, and the man said, "That's a strange way to run a police station."

They found Sergeant Mulholland seated at his usual table, a partly finished pint of Guinness in front of him, reading the paper.

"Sergeant, may we have a word please?" the German man said.

"God give me peace," Mulholland said to himself, "what am I now – a fecking tour guide?"

"Of course," he said politely, "what can I do for you?"

"We wanted to hand in this mobile telephone. We found it at a lay-by by the side of the road between here and Roundstone earlier today," he said.

"Whereabouts exactly was that then?" Mulholland asked.

"I'm not sure, but about five kilometres before Ballyconneely I think, just as the road turns inland for a while, away from the coast. It was in the bushes making a beeping noise because the battery was giving up."

"Oh, right so, well thanks for handing it in. I'll look after it now," Mulholland said, anxious to get back to his pint.

Chapter Six

Thursday, 8:40 am

When Hays arrived at the station the next morning Maureen Lyons was already at her desk. She was studying Dr Dodd's report on the victim, noting that he had found no traces of needle marks on the girl's body, and no trace of opiates in the stomach contents or blood samples.

"How does a respectable girl like that end up dead in a ditch in bloody Connemara?" she said to no one in particular.

"Oh, there'll be a story behind it, wait till you see. There always is," replied Hays.

Flynn and O'Connor arrived together clutching cardboard coffee cups from The Insomnia across the road from the station.

"What's on today, Boss?" Flynn enquired, but before Hays could answer, the phone on his desk began to ring.

"Hays," he said to the caller. When he had listened for a moment he shouted, "What! For fuck sake, Séan, why didn't you call me last night?" He waited a moment for Séan Mulholland's response.

"Now listen here. You get that phone into the squad car and turn on your little blue lights and drive like your life depended on it. I want that phone here by ten o'clock this morning, do you hear? No excuses." He slammed down the receiver. "God give me strength," he sighed to the curious onlookers.

"It seems a mobile phone was discovered not far from the place the girl's body was found. It was handed in to Mulholland last night by two German hikers, but he couldn't be arsed to let us know," Hays said. "Anyway," he went on, calming down a little, "it may not be connected, but we need to get it here and have the lab go over it."

The phone on his desk rang again.

"This is the front desk, Inspector. There's a man here who wants to see the officer in charge of the missing girl case," the desk sergeant said.

"Righto, show him into the interview room, I'll be there right away."

"Maureen, I need you with me," he said, nodding his head in the direction of the door.

* * *

The man in the interview room sat nervously at the table facing the door.

"Good morning, sir. I believe you are here about the missing girl. Thanks for coming in. What can you tell us?" said Hays as he took a seat opposite him.

The man was in his late thirties or early forties. He was well groomed and neatly dressed in a business suit, and well-polished black leather shoes. He had a long thin face and deep blue eyes with a mop of dark hair going a little grey at the temples.

His accent was West of Ireland, but not strongly so, and he spoke in a soft, quiet voice. "Well, I think I may know her," he said a little shyly.

"You think, or you do know her?" asked Hays.

"Well it's not such a good photograph, but I think it's her, OK. What's happened to her?" he asked.

"Do you know her name?" Lyons asked.

"If it's the girl I'm thinking of, her name is Lisa. That's all I know, I don't have a surname. I think she's Polish," he added.

"I see. And how do you know her, Mr …?" Lyons asked.

"Oh, sorry yes, I'm Liam O'Flaherty. Well it's a bit tricky really. You see I'm married, and well, you know…," his voice trailing off without completing the sentence.

"No, Mr O'Flaherty, I'm afraid we don't know. Why don't you tell us?" Hays responded.

"Well, if it's the same girl, she's kind of like… like an escort that I visited a few times. But my wife mustn't know, she'd kill me. She's pregnant with our third, and well, we don't do much anymore if you know what I mean."

Hays looked at Lyons who seemed just as surprised as he was by the revelation.

"I see. And where did you visit the escort girl, Mr O'Flaherty?" Lyons asked.

"Here in Galway. She has an apartment down by the harbour in one of those new blocks."

"Where were you on Tuesday afternoon and evening, Mr O'Flaherty?" Hays said.

"Tuesday. At work, of course till about six, and then I went out to the GAA Club in Oranmore for some training till about half-eight."

"And you'll have witnesses no doubt," Lyons added.

"Yes, of course. Why? What has happened? I just came in because I saw the poster in a shop and thought I recognized her. I haven't been with her in ages. I'm not in any trouble, am I?" he asked.

"How did you get in touch with this Lisa, Mr O'Flaherty?" Hays asked.

"On the internet. There's a web site and she looked really nice, so I called her."

"Do you happen to have her phone number stored in your phone?" Lyons said.

"You must be joking. Angela, my wife, might have found it. No, I called her from the office."

"Look, I need to go now," he went on, "I'm late for work and they'll be wondering where I've got to."

"I think you'd better call in sick, Mr O'Flaherty. I want you to go with Detective Sergeant Lyons now and see if you can find the web page that Lisa was using on one of our computers. Then I want you to show Detective Lyons exactly where the apartment where you met Lisa is located," Hays said.

"And don't worry, we'll keep this between ourselves for now unless there are further developments," Hays said, nodding to Lyons to get started.

O'Flaherty got up from the table looking extremely nervous and followed Maureen Lyons out of the room.

* * *

Maureen Lyons returned to the incident room with a print out of the web page used by Lisa. It was good to see the girl looking alive and well, even if she was scantily dressed. She was a looker to be sure, with long dark hair, a pretty face, and an amazing figure shown to best advantage by her black lacy underwear. On the web page, she was reclining on a single bed, lying on her side, with her arm propping up her head, and pouting slightly as if she was about to kiss the viewer.

"I'm off down the docks with Casanova to find the girl's apartment. Anyone fancy it?" she asked, looking around.

"I'll come with you," Flynn said, "better not to show a uniform for now till we know what's what."

Hays studied the alluring photo of the girl on the printed page that Lyons had stuck up on the whiteboard. *Well at least we have a phone number now.* Pretty girl, he thought to himself.

The phone number on the web page was an 083-number meaning that the phone service was probably provided by Three Ireland.

"John, get onto Three will you, and ask for the records for this number going back, say, three months," Hays said tapping the print out on the board with his pen. "Both incoming and outgoing. And any other details that they can give you – payment type, frequency and so on. And don't let them put you off with all that data protection bullshit. We can have a warrant arranged by eleven o'clock if necessary. But don't tell them it's a murder enquiry, just say it's ongoing investigations."

* * *

At 10:20 Garda Jim Dolan arrived at the station with the small green Nokia in a plastic bag. He had driven in from Clifden as quickly as conditions would allow, hoping for some recognition from the inspector for his efforts. He was out of luck.

"About bloody time!" snapped Hays as he took the bag from Dolan. "And tell Mulholland he owes me one for this."

"I suppose a cup of coffee is out of the question then?" responded Dolan.

"Ah go on, you're all right. Sure, help yourself," Hays replied.

Hays put on a pair of blue latex gloves before taking the phone out of the bag. The battery had gone dead by now, so he searched in his desk drawer for an old Nokia charger to bring the phone back to life. When he connected it, the moving bars for the battery status began to pulse, showing that it was charging. He hoped that there would be no PIN number needed to access the phone, and he decided to leave it on charge for an hour or so before beginning to explore it.

* * *

The block that housed the apartment that Lisa had occupied was clean and fresh. It was close to Jury's Inn down by the docks. As they got out of the car, the salty sea air was blowing up from the quay.

"Nice place," Lyons said to no one in particular. "I bet the rent here isn't cheap."

At the front entrance, the small cluster of bells showed that L Palowski occupied apartment twenty-one on the second floor.

"Is this where you came to see Lisa?" she asked O'Flaherty.

"Yes, this is it."

"Right. You can go off to work now then, Mr O'Flaherty. But don't leave town. We will need you to make a statement later on, and we may have some more questions for you to answer."

O'Flaherty vanished immediately, skulking off down the street in case anyone might see him.

The front entrance to the block was open, so the two Gardaí entered and made their way up the stairs to the second floor. Flynn knocked loudly on the door of number twenty-one and stood back from the door leaning against the metal bannister opposite.

When there was no reply, he knocked again, but still no one answered.

He looked at Lyons. "Probable cause?"

Lyons nodded, and then to her surprise, instead of booting the door open, Flynn took out a set of about thirty keys from his jacket and started trying them one by one in the apartment door.

"Jaysus Eamon," Lyons said. Flynn just looked at her and shrugged.

The apartment was immaculately clean and tidy inside, if somewhat sparsely furnished. Lyons recognised several items that had come from IKEA. There was a beige sofa opposite the mock fireplace in the living room-cum-kitchen, a rug on the wood effect floor and a small collection of paperbacks on a shelf beside the fireplace. On the shelf there was a head and shoulders photo of the dead girl, happy, smiling for the camera.

The apartment had two bedrooms. One was cosily furnished with a dresser, bedside locker with a lamp, and a single bed made up with a duvet in a pink floral cover and matching pillow. A small brown teddy bear was relaxing in the bed under the duvet with just its head peeping out. A modern white wardrobe with a full-length mirror on the door completed the picture.

The other bedroom was at the back of the apartment block, and although it had a window that looked out onto the courtyard, the room was dark compared to the rest of the flat. By contrast, this room was almost totally bare. There was a four-foot bed with just a single fitted blue sheet on it, a small night stand with a cheap lamp and two bottles of baby oil and a box of Kleenex. At the far side of the bed there was a round plastic waste paper basket that was about half full of discarded tissues. The room smelled of sex, and it was clear that this was Lisa's work room where she entertained her clients.

"We need to get the lab boys down here to do a thorough sweep of the place. Emphasis on the business bedroom – DNA, fingerprints, hair, anything else they can find," Lyons said.

"Will you wait here till they arrive? I'm going back to check in with Mick," she said to Flynn.

Chapter Seven

Thursday, 11:30 am

The little Nokia was sufficiently charged to allow Hays to turn it on. Using a new pair of vinyl gloves he switched it on and heard the familiar Nokia welcome tune. The first thing he did was to check the number of the phone against the number given on Lisa's web page, and it matched, so at least he knew that this was definitely her phone.

He carried it carefully over to John O'Connor's desk.

"You need to keep gloves on, and don't handle it more than you have to. There could still be a useful print or two on it. Copy down a list of all incoming calls for the last week and note the day, time and duration of the call. Copy out any text messages from that time too. Then get it over to forensics for fingerprinting," Hays said.

At one o'clock Hays called the team together for a catch up. He brought them all up to date with the news about the mobile phone, the location of the apartment and what Lyons and Flynn had found there.

"Persons of interest, Maureen – what have we got?" he asked.

"Ciara O'Sullivan who found the body. Not a very likely suspect, and you've already checked her out, Boss. Then there's O'Flaherty. Probably just a punter. He came to us, but even so, there may be more to it. I'd like to see what else we can find on him. That's about it till we get the details off her phone. Oh, and the website might give us a few more if there's a booking feature on it, or an email."

The phone rang on Hays' desk.

When he had finished the call, he spoke to the group. "That was forensics. They want me down at the apartment. Maureen, let's go. John, keep working on the mobile. See if you can get any names from the numbers or the contact list. We'll be back before five for the next briefing," Hays said.

On the way down to the docks in the car, Hays asked Lyons how she thought the case was going so far.

"Not great, to be honest. We've only just identified the girl, and God knows how many potential suspects her line of business will produce. What does the Super think?"

"He's hopping from one foot to the other as usual. He wants to see me tomorrow evening for a progress report, and he emphasised the word 'progress'."

"Let's hope we have something positive to tell him by then."

"You have a good nose for these things, Maureen. Any instincts shouting at you yet?"

"C'mon Mick, it's a bit early for that. But it's looking like a punter to me. Maybe she was blackmailing one of the great and the good of Galway, although what she was doing out there in Ballyconneely is anybody's guess. That's the bit that has me puzzled."

When they got to the apartment, a girl in a full white lab suit approached them, and pulling her hood off to reveal a shock of curly blonde hair and a pretty face said, "Morning, Sergeant. We found a few things that I'd like you to see."

"What have you got, Siobhán?" he asked.

The girl held up two see-through plastic evidence bags. "There's a Credit Union pass book in the name of Lisa Palowski. It shows she has just under fourteen thousand euro on deposit. There are regular weekly lodgements into the account of five hundred euro every Friday in cash," she said, handing the first of the two bags to Hays.

"Then there's this," she said holding up the other plastic bag. "The original little black book. I'll let you examine it for yourself. Looks interesting. Oh, and it was well hidden in her knicker drawer in her own bedroom," the girl added.

"Well done, Siobhán, that's great. Anything else of interest?"

"The bed in the spare room has been very well used, and the waste paper basket has some interesting specimens, but it will take a day or two to get anything useful."

"I don't envy you that one," said Lyons. "Can we take these away with us?"

"Yes sure. They have been catalogued and dusted so they're all yours. Do you want the contents of the bin too when we're done with it?"

"It's OK thanks, you can keep that," Lyons said, rolling her eyes to heaven.

On the way back to the station in the car, Lyons started studying the little black Moleskine notebook.

It wasn't originally a diary, but Lisa had made it into one by putting the day and date at the top of each page and putting the hours in a neat clear hand down the left-hand side. It was marked up in this way for several weeks ahead and seemed to go back about two months in time. There were no pages for Sundays, and Lyons noted that there was a whole week missing every four weeks or so, reflecting, presumably, the days she was unable to work due to mother nature.

The working days had initials or first names written in alongside the time. A typical day had one or two appointments, but some days had three, spread out from eleven in the morning to ten at night. Two or three of the names appeared quite regularly, every ten days or so. Lisa, probably without knowing it, had kept meticulous records of her clients that would surely prove invaluable in tracking down her killer.

"If I ever decide to go on the game instead of enforcing law and order, I can use this as a template. The pay looks great, and don't forget it's all tax free."

"Well let me know, won't you? I can be your first client," Hays said as he looked across at Maureen and smiled.

* * *

Back at the station, Hays called the team together.

"We have some good information from the girl's flat now. We need to cross-reference the diary to the phone records and see if we can identify any of Lisa's clients. It looks like James was the last one to have an appointment with her at four o'clock on Tuesday afternoon. Let's see if we can identify James, if that's his real name," Hays said.

Another hour of searching and cross-referencing went by quickly, and when Hays called them back together again, there was some good news.

"So, how goes it with the phone records?" he asked.

Flynn who had been coordinating the cross-referencing spoke up.

"Most of the calls are from pay-as-you-go mobiles, and of course none of them are registered, so they are anonymous. There is one thing we spotted though. About two weeks ago she had an appointment with this James at five o'clock. Earlier that day she got a call from a landline here in the city. I called the number, and it was answered by a receptionist at a firm of architects on Dominick Street." He paused for effect.

"Well come on man, what's the name of these architects then?" Hays said impatiently.

"They're called McMahon and O'Reilly. And the McMahon in question is one James McMahon!"

An audible hum of excitement went around the room.

"Great work, Eamon, well done all of you. This is our first solid lead. Now we need to be very careful here. Let's see if we can identify James' mobile from calls made about the same time on other days when she saw him. And I don't want any contact with him till we are good and ready. Is that understood?"

"Yes, Boss," they echoed in unison.

"Dig up all you can on this guy. I want to know more about him than he knows about himself before we talk to him. What car does he drive? Where does he live? Is he married? Family? What clubs does he belong to? Who his friends are, and above all if he is well-connected around town, although that's probably a 'yes' if he's an architect."

"Let's convene at nine-thirty in the morning with whatever you've got."

"Maureen, can you stay back for a few minutes please?" Hays added.

"Sure, no problem," she said, moving towards Hays' private office.

"Would you like a coffee?" Hays asked.

"No, I'm fine thanks, it only keeps me awake if I have it at this time of day. What's on your mind?"

"You know I think highly of you. We've worked on some pretty tricky stuff together in the past. I just wanted to get your gut feel for what we're getting into with this Lisa Palowski thing. I haven't worked this type of case before, and I don't have a feel for it yet."

"I know what you mean, it's kind of uncharted waters for me too. But look at it this way. What she was doing was what you might call a high-risk occupation. Now I know that's not a good reason to whack her over the head with a rock, but in that line of work there's always a risk of violence, and there's no one around to protect you either unless you have a pimp, which she doesn't appear to have had. Oh, and another thing, if we find this James is well connected, then we really will have to tread very carefully. In this town, whatever he has done, he's likely to get more sympathy than an Eastern European escort from the powers that be. And what I can't figure out at all, is what she was doing out there. It doesn't add up. Someone must have driven her out there, or maybe she drove herself, but in that case, where's the car?"

"Let's see what tomorrow brings shall we," she said. "Are you OK?" "What. Oh yes, sorry, I'm fine, just processing what you were saying. Let's watch each other's backs, eh?"

"Of course. And anytime you want to talk, you know," she added.

"Oh yes, thanks. See you tomorrow."

Hays dawdled around in the office for a little while longer. He was just about to head home when his phone rang. It was Ciara O'Sullivan.

"Inspector, oh I'm glad I caught you. I was on my way home when I saw a small poster in a shop window. It's her, isn't it, the girl I found out at Ballyconneely?"

"Yes, that's her. What's up?"

"Well, I think I know her, in fact I'm sure I do. Her name is Lisa. We were in college together, and we ran an event for charity before she stopped attending."

"I see. How come you didn't tell us this before, Ciara, it could be important?"

"Well I didn't recognise her in the dark, and the condition she was in. But it's her, isn't it? Oh God, this is terrible."

"Were you in touch with her recently?" Hays asked.

"No, not for ages. I may as well tell you, you'll find out in any case. We had a row. I was going with a boy from college, and she kind of took him from me. I was pretty upset at the time, I thought he loved me. But I'm over it all now for ages."

"What was this lad's name?" Hays asked.

"Brian, Brian Leddy."

"Are you still in touch with him at all?"

"No. He finished college same time as me, and he went to Australia I think. I haven't seen him for ages."

"And there's definitely nothing more you want to tell me, Ciara?"

"No, no, of course not," she said.

"Well, OK. You'll have to come in and amend your statement at some stage, and we may need to speak to you again. You're not planning any holidays, are you?"

"No, no, of course not. When do you want me to come in?" she asked.

"We'll be in touch, Ciara."

"Oh, OK. If you want to see me, just give me a call. I'll give you my mobile number." She called out her number which Hays wrote down on his notepad.

After the phone call, Hays finally left and drove home to his house in Salthill. Although he was very self-sufficient, managing his domestic affairs with ease – the mundane matters of keeping his clothes fresh, stocking the larder, cooking and keeping the house in some sort of basic order – he was lonely all the same. He had never known the welcoming smile of a wife or partner, nor the chaos and noise that a family of young children bring to a home. Although he convinced himself that he was fine, he knew deep down that his solitary life was missing a lot of potential happiness that sharing can bring.

Chapter Eight

Friday, 9:00 am

Hays and Lyons were both in early and had spent some time going over the information on James McMahon.

McMahon was a successful architect who had set up practice in Galway some twelve years ago. He had timed it well. Galway was undergoing a mini-boom all of its own, and there were lots of projects involving the refurbishment of old buildings, hotels, and pubs, as well as a good number of new-build offices going up.

McMahon, together with his junior colleague Brian O'Reilly had quickly established the practice as the "go to" firm for all things architectural. The practice expanded rapidly, and now employed twelve people – a mixture of draughtsmen, quantity surveyors and junior architects, as well as a compliance officer and of course the inevitable pretty twenty-three-year-old receptionist and an equally pretty female office manager.

McMahon was a native of Athenry. His parents were farmers and machinery contractors and were fairly well heeled. When he had completed his Leaving Certificate, McMahon had been sent off to Bolton Street College in Dublin to learn his trade at the age of nineteen. During the four years that he was studying, he stayed with an uncle and aunt in Raheny, and pursued a pretty good social life while making sure that he came near the top of the class in his exams.

Armed with his new qualification, at twenty-three he moved to England and entered the building trade. He was soon buying 'fixer-uppers' and doing them up, selling them on at serious profit which allowed him to amass a goodly amount of precious Sterling.

Soon after returning to Galway, he had built a very spacious house out by Kilcornan Wood a few miles outside the city on the road that had later become known as 'millionaires row'.

Along the way he married a Galway girl, and between them they had produced two children, a boy and a girl. He had also become a leading light in the Galway Lions Club which allowed him to share some of his considerable fortune with the less well-off and was also very helpful to him in a business sense.

"We're going to have to tread really carefully here. This guy is connected. God knows who he is in with. I think I'll run this past the Super before we go charging in," Hays said.

"Have a look and see if there is any record at all of any interaction with us. Any signs of previous violence towards women in particular. Oh, and check with the UK too, they may have something. Then maybe we'll go and have a wee chat with our friendly architect."

Lyons dug around in the Pulse database but could find nothing at all on McMahon. He appeared to be squeaky clean. She then called a contact that she had in the Met in London and asked her to have a snoop around to see if there was anything there.

Hays returned twenty minutes later having spoken to the superintendent about James McMahon.

"He said to go ahead and interview McMahon but go easy. The Super knows him from the Lions, and says he can be quite prickly," Hays said. "Are you up for it?"

"Sure, no bother. Might as well get fired for upsetting one of the Super's mates as anything else. I never really liked this job anyway," she said, smiling at Hays.

* * *

The offices of McMahon and O'Reilly – written with a plus sign on an aluminium plate outside the building – were ultra-modern with lots of glass, grey marble and brushed metal on display. The building itself was tall and narrow, and occupied three floors in a courtyard just off Dominick Street.

The front door opened onto a small reception area with a desk and a comfortable-looking black leather sofa packed in between two tall indoor plants that looked rather thirsty. The pretty receptionist was seated behind the desk and a name plate indicated that her name was Irene Weir.

"Hello Irene. We are here to see Mr McMahon. My name is Inspector Hays and this is Sergeant Lyons from Galway Garda," he said, holding out his warrant card.

Irene seemed only slightly fazed by their request, and responded as they assumed she would: "I'm afraid Mr McMahon is in conference with a client at the moment, but they'll be finished soon. He has another meeting in fifteen minutes," Irene said in quite a posh, but genuine, local accent.

Boarding school, Maureen thought to herself.

"Can I get you a coffee while you're waiting?" she asked.

"Thank you. Two white coffees no sugar," Hays replied, and the two detectives took up their seats beside each other on the leather couch.

The coffee was good – nice and hot, and not bitter, but the drink was let down a little by the thick white mugs with 'McMahon + O'Reilly' printed on them in which it was served. No biscuits were offered. Maureen assumed that they were reserved for paying clients and not mere police.

At five minutes to eleven a thick and solid cherrywood door at the end of the reception area opened and three men emerged. It quickly became obvious that the two in front were the clients, and the man standing behind them ushering them out of the office was McMahon.

When he had seen his clients out, he turned quizzically to Irene as if to say, "Who the hell are these two?"

McMahon was tall, probably six-one or six-two, slim with neatly trimmed salt and pepper hair and a tanned angular face. He was dressed in an immaculate and expensive grey suit which fitted him perfectly, set off with a pristine blue shirt and an expensive silk tie.

He approached the two Gardaí who by now were standing, extending his hand towards Lyons.

"Good morning folks. What can I do for you today? Wife been parking on double yellow lines again!" he said with a smirk.

"Could we have a few minutes of your time in private please, Mr McMahon?" Hays asked.

"Sure, come into my office. I haven't got long though, I have another appointment at eleven," he said.

Hays gave Lyons a look that said, "We'll see about that," and they went on into the office.

The office was quite sparse. McMahon's desk was a little too large for the room. He sat with his back to the window, facing the door. A glass-fronted bookcase was filled with architectural texts, and a framed certificate on the wall confirmed McMahon's status as a member of the Royal Institute of the Architects of Ireland, RIAI for short.

Against the only remaining wall stood a chest with ten shallow, wide drawers which looked as if it was used to house architectural drawings. On top of the chest was an old theodolite, all brass and lenses, which presumably was just for decoration.

His desk had a photograph of the man himself with a blonde woman of about his own age and two small children of maybe five and seven. There was a modern telephone, a small stack of trays for papers, and a diary, but no sign of any files or drawings.

McMahon gestured the two detectives to sit in front of his desk.

"Now, what's all this about?" McMahon asked.

Lyons opened the proceedings.

"May we ask where you were on Tuesday afternoon, between say three and seven, Mr McMahon?" she asked.

McMahon flicked the diary back a page or two and consulted it.

"Actually, no," he mused, "I wasn't in the office on Tuesday. I remember now. I had to go and see a client at the Golf Club. We had a meeting at four-thirty."

"And which Golf Club would that be?" Hays interjected.

"I'm a member out at the Connemara club near Ballyconneely, you know it I'm sure."

"And did you meet your client?"

"Actually, no. He didn't turn up. The weather was really bad. Lashing rain and wind. In fact the place was more or less deserted," McMahon responded.

"So, what did you do then?" Lyons asked.

"I had a cup of coffee at the bar. Tried to call him, but there was no signal. I hung around for about three quarters of an hour in case he turned up, and then drove back to town."

"Did anyone see you there?" Hays said.

"No, as I say, the place was pretty well deserted, except for Liam at the bar of course. He served me."

"And what time did you get back to town then?" Lyons asked.

"It must have been around six-ish. I remember the traffic was awful. I came back to the office and did a few hours before I went home."

"Can anyone confirm that you were here at that time?" Lyons asked.

"Of course not. They all go home at five-thirty. Look, what's this about?" he said looking at his watch.

"Do you know a girl called Lisa Palowski?" Lyons said.

"No, I don't recall the name. Who is she?"

"Are you sure, Mr McMahon?"

"I said I didn't know her, didn't I? Do you not believe me?" he snapped. He was becoming quite agitated now just as Lyons had hoped he would.

"May I see your mobile phone please, Mr McMahon?" Lyons persisted.

McMahon reached into his jacket pocket which was now draped over the back of his chair and fished out an iPhone six which he handed to Lyons, protesting all the way.

"This is getting silly. I've answered your questions. I'm extremely busy today and my next appointment will be waiting in reception. Have you quite finished?"

Lyons had given the phone to Hays who was scrolling down through the call history and contacts looking for Lisa's number. He caught Lyons' eye and shook his head slightly.

"Not quite, Mr McMahon. If you prefer we could continue down at the station," Hays paused for a moment and went on, "with your lawyer present."

Hays reached unobserved into the side pocket of his jacket and pressed the green button on the front of Lisa's Nokia. Almost at once the muffled sound of a mobile phone began to chirp.

The phone rang three times before Lyons said, "Aren't you going to answer that, Mr McMahon?"

McMahon went red in the face. He opened the top drawer of his desk and took out a small black phone and looked at the screen, which clearly identified the caller as Lisa.

Hays took the Nokia out of his pocket and held it up for McMahon to see. He pressed the red button on the phone and the incessant chirping stopped.

"Now, Mr McMahon, we can do this one of two ways. I can arrest you here and now on suspicion of the murder of Lisa Palowski. That gives us the right to search these premises, your home, and seize your vehicle for forensic testing. All very public and quite unpleasant for your family and employees. Or you can agree to come in voluntarily, provide a DNA sample, and start helping us with our enquiries and stop lying to us. Which is it to be?" Hays said.

"Look, yes I lied about knowing Lisa. But you have to understand, you know what she is. I have my reputation to think of, my standing in the community. And Jennifer – good God what would she think? I'll tell you the truth. I'll cooperate. I never harmed the girl, I swear," he stuttered, all of his composure gone.

"Mr James McMahon, I'm arresting you on suspicion of…" Hays began.

"No. No. Don't do that. I'll come with you. I'll do whatever you want, just keep it low key for heaven's sake!" McMahon interrupted.

"Right then. Get your things. Maureen, bag up the black phone please, it's evidence. And bring your diary please, Mr McMahon, we need that," Hays said.

McMahon's next appointment was waiting in the reception. He apologised to the man, saying that something urgent had come up, and Irene would re-arrange another appointment.

The receptionist was aghast at seeing her boss departing with the two Gardaí, but kept her composure and said nothing.

On the way back to the station Lyons engaged James McMahon in conversation about his architectural practice. She pointed out a few buildings and allowed him to prattle on about the work he had done on them. This was her way of interrupting his thoughts so that he couldn't spend the time weaving another story to try and get himself out of the hole he was in. It worked too. The man was vain and delighted in telling Lyons all about his massive achievements around the town.

* * *

The team got together once again in the incident room. Lyons had already posted a photo of James McMahon on the board, which now had three pictures – Lisa Palowski, Ciara O'Sullivan and James McMahon.

Hays addressed the group. "Before we get started on McMahon, I had a phone call from Ciara O'Sullivan last night just before I left. It turns out she knew Lisa Palowski too, from college. Seems they had a row over some college stud, so she may not be as innocent as she seems, though Dodd did say that Lisa had been hit by a man. O'Sullivan is pretty tall though, so you never know. I need a volunteer to go over to Hynes' Yard car park and have a look at her car, see if there's any damage. John, could you do that while we deal with McMahon – her reg. number is on file?"

"Sure, Boss, I'll head over there now."

"Right guys, we need to get busy now with this. McMahon is here voluntarily, and he'll be itching to get home in a few hours, so we haven't got long, unless we arrest him," Hays said.

"John, before you go, will you get on to Sergeant Mulholland and ask him to drive out to the Connemara Golf Club? He's looking to interview Liam, the barman. See if he remembers McMahon being there on Tuesday around half-past four. Get Mulholland to take a statement, and ask him to do it now, not later, and not tomorrow. He can phone it in when he has some news," Hays said.

"Oh, and when you've done that, get back to Lisa's phone company. See if they have managed to dig up any more of her contacts from the numbers in her phone."

"Eamon, will you and Maureen go and interview McMahon? Get him to give up a DNA sample, and fingerprints. See if you can get his car keys too," Hays added.

"I'll go and update the boss, and get forensics working on the vehicle when we get hold of it. Let's meet back at four – and we need some results."

* * *

Flynn and Lyons spent over an hour grilling James McMahon. He had refused a solicitor on the grounds that he had nothing to hide, and in any case his lawyer was a family friend, and he didn't want to involve him at this stage for obvious reasons.

At three-thirty they took a comfort break, McMahon demanding the right to go home as he had nothing more to say. He had stuck to his story about driving out to Ballyconneely to meet a client on Tuesday.

During the short recess Lyons' phone rang. "This is Mulholland here, Sergeant," he boomed. "I did as you asked. I drove out to the golf club and spoke to Liam, the guy behind the bar. He told me that there was no one at all in the place Tuesday afternoon. The weather was dreadful, so bad that he locked up at about half past three and went home. But he was certain that there had been no one at all in the bar that day," Mulholland reported triumphantly.

"Thanks, Sergeant," Lyons said and hurried off to find Hays with the news.

"I see," said Hays. "This changes things quite a bit. I'd better come down with you myself now. We may need to charge him."

"Well Mr McMahon," Hays said addressing the man in a serious tone. "It seems you have been spinning us a right old yarn, so it does."

McMahon started to say something but Hays held up his palm to silence him before continuing.

"It appears that you've been telling us a right load of lies about your whereabouts on Tuesday afternoon. You weren't at the golf club in Ballyconneely at all were you?" Hays demanded. He let the question hang in the air. McMahon looked him dead in the eyes and waited for a full thirty seconds before replying.

"Why do you say that?" he asked.

"Look Mr McMahon, I don't think you really understand the seriousness of your situation. You have fed us some tall story about where you were when the girl was murdered. You had the opportunity, almost certainly the means, and I can easily guess the motive," Hays went on.

Holding up his forefinger and thumb barely a centimetre apart, Hays said, "I'm just that close to charging you with the murder of Lisa Palowski, and unless you start telling me the entire truth within the next five minutes, that's exactly what I will do."

Another silence – shorter this time.

"All right, all right. I was with the girl on Tuesday. I went to her apartment at four o'clock and spent an hour with her. But I swear, when I left her she was fit and healthy, you have to believe me," he said in desperation.

"Wrong, Mr McMahon, we don't have to believe you at all. And after all the lies you've told us it's now up to you to prove what you're saying is true," Hays said.

Lyons cut in. "What happened? Did she threaten to expose you? Did she demand a lot of money? You lost your temper didn't you and whacked her about the head then put the body in the car and drove it out west towards Clifden and dumped it. Isn't that right, Mr McMahon?"

"No, no. Not at all. We parted on good terms. She even asked me when I would see her again. She wouldn't threaten me, she wasn't like that. Despite her chosen career, she was a nice girl underneath. She had standards. We liked each other. I even brought her a present back from Frankfurt earlier this year. I was over there at an architectural conference."

"Yes, a gold bangle," Lyons said. "She was wearing it when we found her."

"So how come this nice escort girl ended up dead in a ditch forty miles from home just a few hours after you were with her, Mr McMahon?" Hays said, getting back on track.

"I don't know. I don't bloody know. Maybe she had another visitor after I left her, I don't know."

"Let me tell you this, Mr McMahon, if we find just one tiny trace of her anywhere in your car, that's it, I'll do you for her murder," Hays said.

McMahon leant forward and put his head in his hands. After a few moments he said, "You will find traces of her. Only in the front passenger's seat though. I drove her around a bit sometimes when she had stuff to get, you know, shopping and that."

Hays signalled to Lyons that they needed to talk outside in private.

"Stay put for the moment, we'll be back shortly," he said.

Outside in the corridor, Hays asked Lyons, "What do you think? Is he our man?"

"You don't think so, do you?" Lyons replied.

"I don't know. So, he sees a hooker. He's scared to death anyone will find out. He lied to us, but I don't see him killing the girl, do you?"

"Well when it boils down to it, we haven't got that much on him. And after all it was he who placed himself in the vicinity with that bullshit about the golf club. He wouldn't have done that if he had dumped her out there. We'll know more when we have had a look at the car. Where did he say he went after he had been with the girl on Tuesday?"

"Back to the office. Says he got there about half five or quarter to six, but by that time everyone had gone home," Hays replied.

"Why don't I go back to his office with him and see if I can get the login records from his PC for Tuesday, see if he logged back in when he said he did?" Lyons asked.

"Good idea. Then let him go for now. Tell him not to leave Galway, oh and tell him we'll be keeping his car for a few days. He can tell the wife it's in the garage."

"Oh, and Maureen, can you come back here after? There's a few things I'd like to go over with you," he added.

"Yeah sure. I'll see you later then."

* * *

Lyons arrived back at the station having escorted McMahon to his office.

"Hi Boss. It looks as if he may be in the clear. We got the log off his PC, and true enough he logged back in at five forty-two and stayed logged in till after eight. There were a number of emails and documents created in that time, so I don't think he was faking it."

"Probably genuine," Hays said. "It would be very difficult to set that up as an alibi, after all he didn't know he was a suspect till this morning, and we have been with him ever since."

"But I don't want him ruled out of the picture just yet. There's a good bit of circumstantial linking him in, and he's a clever bugger, so he could be spinning all sorts of yarns. There's no doubt he's shit scared that anyone will find out his dirty little secret. Maybe this will put an end to his afternoon delights for the time being," Hays said.

"What about the girl that found the body – the fragrant Ciara?" Lyons asked.

"I'm not sure we should prioritize her. Let's have a think about it over the weekend and see what develops. No harm if you called on her and had a chat next week maybe, see what you can worm out of her, but to be honest, I doubt if she'd commit murder just to avenge a stolen boyfriend that happened a few years ago, but we'll check it out just to be sure," Hays said.

"I've had enough of this for today. Do you fancy a drink?" he added.

"Yes please. I could do with a nice cold G and T, or maybe two." She smiled at Hays.

* * *

Doherty's Bar and Lounge was the nearest decent pub to the station. It had been given a hefty makeover in 2010 and now looked more like a 1950s boozer than anything modern. Shelves around the walls, up high, were adorned with old books, a couple of old valve radios, and a few ancient kitchen utensils in copper and brass. The lounge was comfortable, with carpet, and the seating was arranged in a series of semi-private booths separated by trellis that had been painted dark brown. A long mahogany bar ran the length of the room with every imaginable concoction anyone could want on tap, or in bottles.

Hays waited at the bar for his pint of Guinness to settle while Tadgh Doherty poured Maureen's Bombay Sapphire Gin – a double measure and a little "tilly" as well and added the Schweppes tonic water. Tadgh knew just how she liked it, with a slice of lime, not lemon, and two cubes of ice.

Back in their booth, Hays raised his glass. "Sláinte," he said, and Maureen reciprocated in time-honoured fashion.

"Maureen, I know tomorrow is Saturday and all that, but I was wondering if I could ask a favour?" Hays said.

"Saturday is just the day after Friday, Boss. Go ahead."

"I feel we're spinning our wheels a bit on this one. It's nearly a week now, and we're not really anywhere," he said.

"The boss is going mad. He's getting real heat from Dublin 8, and he's afraid they'll send some of their sharp shooters down from the smoke to take over if we don't make more progress really soon. He'd really hate that. It would be a terrible insult to him and us."

"Damn right," Lyons said, "anyway they have enough murders going on in Dublin to keep them busy," she hissed.

"So, I'd like us, just you and me, to go back out to the place where she was found early tomorrow morning. I don't know why, but I have a feeling that there's something out there that we may have missed. I know it's a long shot, and I don't like asking, but it could be useful if you're up for it," he said.

"It's been well covered by the forensic boys and girls, but I suppose they did come up with bugger all. They might have missed something. Anyway, what's a poor young detective sergeant doing on a Saturday morning if she's not driving around the wild west with her boss!"

"Thanks, I appreciate it. You have a great nose for this kind of thing, and in the peace of the morning out there we might get a better feel for what went on," he said.

"What about O'Sullivan's car? Did John find anything?" Lyons asked.

"Not a thing. Says it's clean as a whistle, no damage on it anywhere. Still doesn't mean she's not involved. I don't like coincidences," he said. "She could have met Lisa in the city and offered her a lift out west for some reason, and then when she got her out into the wilderness stopped the car and started a row about the boyfriend. It could have got out of hand. Who knows?" Hays said.

He went on, "Remind me to get Dolan to check with the curtain lady tomorrow. If Lisa had been in O'Sullivan's car, she might have seen her, and that would explain why she didn't want to stop for tea and cake."

"All seems a bit unlikely, but not impossible. Do you think she recognised Lisa the night she was found, if her story is true?"

"Possibly. Hard to tell. If you had been there, you would have been able to tell. You're good at that sort of thing," Hays said.

"Maybe you'll have to interview Ciara again then. She's a right looker, isn't she?" Lyons said, watching Hays carefully for a reaction.

"She is that, all right. Might be better if you questioned her – less complicated."

"Right you are," Lyons responded, somewhat relieved.

"One for the road?" she asked, and catching the eye of Tadgh Doherty, held up her nearly empty glass.

Chapter Nine

Saturday, 8:30 am

Hays buzzed the bell marked 'Lyons' on the outside of the small two storey house on Corrib Terrace where Maureen lived. The house was in good order. It looked onto a park and was just a short stroll to the river while being convenient to the city at the same time.

She had found the little house soon after arriving in Galway. It belonged to a Garda sergeant from Athenry who had inherited it from his mother who passed away in the 1990s. He and a few friends had completely gutted the place which had been stuck well and truly in the 1940s and totally modernised it. It was now set in two one-bedroom flats, and Maureen occupied the upper floor. It had a good-sized bedroom overlooking the park, a kitchen and living room to the back, and a small bathroom with a shower tucked in between.

The door phone crackled to life, and Maureen said, "Hi. Come on up, I'm just about ready."

The door buzzed allowing Hays in to the small hallway, and up the stairs to Maureen's door which she had left ajar for him.

Maureen, still in her cotton pyjamas that surprisingly showed off her neat size ten figure quite well, was at the kitchen counter.

"Coffee?" she asked, turning to Hays with a jar of Nescafé in one hand and a spoon in the other.

"Yes please. One spoon and just a splash of milk."

"I'm much nearer to being ready than I look," she smiled, handing him a mug of hot coffee that bore the legend "I Love Galway," with the word 'Love' represented by a big red heart.

Hays could smell the fragrance of whatever shower gel she had used and couldn't help but admire the curve of her breasts as she leaned forward to give him the drink.

"Two minutes," she said, disappearing into the bedroom. Hays thought to himself that the view from the back was just as delightful. Did she know the effect she was having on him? Yes, he mused, women always know.

When Maureen emerged from the bedroom, she looked even better than she had done in her pyjamas. She was wearing an extremely well-cut pair of denim jeans that fitted perfectly, a cream polo shirt and had a navy fleece with no sleeves to finish the ensemble. Her hair, usually in a ponytail, was now loose around her head, and her make-up was absolutely perfect, making her look a good five years younger than she did at the office.

"What?" she said, smiling as she noticed Hays staring a little.

He just smiled back and said nothing.

* * *

It was a pleasant drive out through Moycullen and Oughterard. The day was brightening up, the Twelve Pins in the distance looked magnificent in their 'Paul Henry Blue', and the high cotton wool clouds set off against the blue sky completed the picture postcard scene. In Oughterard some of the houses already had their fires going, and the blue sweet-smelling smoke of burning turf rose vertically from several chimneys. The town was beginning to stir, but traffic was light. They crossed the bridge, and drove out past the now closed McSweeneys Hotel, along the banks of the fast-flowing river that ran beside the road, before it rose up out of the town onto the top of the peat bog.

When they had cleared Oughterard, Hays said to Maureen, "So how are you getting on with everything at the station?"

"Oh, it's fine. I enjoy the work. Thank God there aren't too many murders in Galway. One a year is enough for any girl. It gets a bit boring sometimes, but that's OK too."

"Do you do anything in the evenings these days?" he enquired.

"Well I was thinking of starting Spanish lessons this autumn, but I missed the start date of the course, so I guess I'll have to wait till next year now."

"Why Spanish?"

"I just love the country. It has so much variety. I don't mean the madness of Ibiza or Magaluf, I did all that shit when I was a teenager. But on the mainland, Madrid, Toledo, Salamanca, even Granada and Seville, all those places are so beautiful and steeped in history."

"Would you ever think of living there?"

"Nah. It's not for me. I'm a Galway girl through and through, but I'd love to spend the winter months touring around that part of Spain north of Madrid. Get away from Ireland's miserable weather."

"So, you won't be joining the Guardia Civil anytime soon then?" he teased.

"Not likely."

"Talking of which, have you thought about going forward for inspector at all?"

"It's too soon. You have to be an old fogey to be an inspector in Galway," she said, nudging his leg in a playful way. "And besides, I like working with you. You treat me well, but there's still that fine line where you are definitely the boss. I like that."

"I see. You're a bit of a sub then."

"No, I wouldn't say that. I can take charge in all kinds of situations. I can even be quite bossy. But I like knowing that you're covering my back if I fuck up. I wouldn't have that if we were of equal rank."

"Just make sure you don't fuck up, Sergeant!" They laughed out loud together.

They turned off the N59 just after Recess, and meandered into Roundstone, passing the Anglers' Return nestled in the little copse of trees down by the river where the trout fishing went on in season, and on out past the old wooden bridge that led to Inishnee. Roundstone was still asleep as they drove through past the church and the Garda station that was closed on Saturday.

They passed Dog's Bay, looking magnificent as ever, with the sun glinting on the snow-white beach, and the water a clear crystal blue, glistening in the morning sun. A few stray rabbits bounded around, darting this way and that. The place was deserted at this time of day, and Hays would have liked to have stopped and walked out along the headland to the point. He loved this place. But they pressed on along the old bog road till they reached the little bridge where Lisa Palowski had been found by Ciara O'Sullivan just a few days earlier. Hays pulled in and parked about thirty metres short of the spot.

"What are we looking for?" Lyons asked.

"Anything at all. Follow your nose. Let the scene talk to you."

The two detectives walked around the site slowly. Hays went well off the road into the boggy, rocky heath where the reeds grew tall and brown, and sheep eked out a meagre meal on the patchy grass. The ground squelched under his feet, and his shoes were starting to let in, making his socks wet.

Lyons stayed by the road, walking up and down along the small stones, staring down into the murky brown bog water that formed a semi-stagnant stream all along by the roadside. About twenty-five feet short of the bridge she stooped down, and put her left hand into the bog water almost up to her elbow. It was slightly brown and a little slimy, but she had seen something all the same and was determined to retrieve whatever it was. She picked out a small rectangle of soggy cream coloured cardboard about the size of a cigarette packet. She turned it over in her hand to find she was looking at the stub of a Ryanair boarding card.

"Mick," she shouted. "Mick, over here. I've got something."

The boarding card yielded a surprising amount of information. The flight was FR1902 from Krakow in

Poland to Dublin. The boarding card stated that travel had taken place the day before Lisa Palowski had been found dead, and the passenger was one Piotr Palowski who sat in seat 24D on the flight.

"Jesus," Hays exclaimed, "how the hell was this missed?"

"Still, well done you, Maureen, I could kiss you," he said.

"That could be fun," she said, but the comment appeared to go unnoticed.

"OK. Let's have another quick look around in the same area, see if there's anything else. Then we'll head back, and I want the full team in the office for one o'clock, Saturday or no Saturday," he said.

* * *

The team was assembled rather grumpily when Hays and Lyons got back to the station.

"Thanks for coming in on Saturday, folks. You know I wouldn't have asked you if it wasn't important," Hays said.

"Maureen and I drove out to where the girl was found this morning, and Maureen found this in the bottom of the ditch near where the girl's body was found," Hays said, holding up the small rectangle of cardboard that Lyons had dried out using the car heater on the way back to town.

"It's a Ryanair boarding card for one Piotr Palowski, who flew to Dublin from Krakow on Monday last," he said.

A surprised murmur went around the room.

"How did the crime scene guys miss that?" Flynn asked. "Do you think it was there all along?"

"Yes, I do. Maureen found it more by instinct than by searching. But we need to get on. This is the first positive lead we have had," Hays replied.

"John, will you get onto Ryanair. Get O'Leary himself if you're not getting anywhere. I want to know everything there is to know about this guy. And particularly if he is still in Ireland. Eamon, can you give John a hand?"

"Yes, sure Boss. I wonder who he is. Husband maybe?" Flynn mused.

"Well that's what we need to find out. I'm going to get on the web, see if I can find him on Facebook or LinkedIn. Try to build a picture. Let's reconvene in an hour."

Ryanair were more helpful than any of them had imagined. Piotr Palowski had flown into Dublin on Monday for a one week stay. He had hired a car for the week through the Ryanair web site and had booked a hotel in Galway. But the story didn't end there. On Tuesday night Wednesday morning, he had logged on and changed his booking to take him back to Krakow on the Wednesday evening flight.

Ryanair were able to provide his address in Krakow from the booking as well as from his credit card details, and they told O'Connor that the car had been supplied by Hertz at Dublin airport.

Hays told O'Connor to get onto Hertz at the airport and get the details of the car hire arrangements.

"Maureen, you and I are going down to Jury's Inn to see what we can find out," Hays said.

"Oh yeah," O'Connor said with a wide grin.

"Behave John, you pervert," Hays responded.

The receptionist at Jury's Inn on Quay Street was a pretty, fair-haired girl dressed in a grey suit and white blouse with a little red bow tie. She too was Polish, and she confirmed that Piotr Palowski had arrived late on Monday night by car, and that he had originally booked in for a week. She also confirmed that he had only stayed two nights and had unexpectedly checked out early on Wednesday.

"What reason did he give for his early departure?" Lyons asked.

"He said something about family issues back in Poland, and said he had to get back urgently. I was on duty, and to be honest, he seemed quite shaken up," the girl replied.

"I don't suppose there's any chance the room hasn't been made up since?" Lyons enquired.

"I'm sorry. Even at this time of year we are pretty full. We were able to re-let his room the same day," she said.

"And I don't suppose there was anything left behind in the room at all?" Lyons added.

"Hold on, I'll check with housekeeping."

Piotr Palowski hadn't left anything behind in his room when he checked out on Wednesday morning. The hotel had charged him an extra night as a cancellation fee, and he hadn't disputed the charge. He just seemed anxious to be underway.

* * *

Back at the station, John O'Connor had been in touch with Hertz at Dublin Airport. They told him that the car that was hired by Piotr Palowski had been returned early on Wednesday afternoon.

"But there's more," he said. "Hertz told me that there was damage to the car when it came back in. The left front wing and headlight were damaged. They have sent it to the repair shop over in Swords."

"Terrific. They won't have cleaned it yet. Get back on to them and find out exactly where it is, the registration number, make and colour of the car. Then get onto the Gardaí in Dublin and ask them to go out and secure the vehicle till we can arrange a forensic examination. Maybe there will be some evidence or perhaps even some blood residue on it," Hays said.

"Maureen, can you get in touch with the police in Krakow? Explain the situation. Get as much information on this guy as they are willing to give you but ask them not to make contact with him yet. We don't want him doing a runner."

"I'm going to call the Super and see what he suggests," Hays said.

* * *

By four o'clock quite a bit of additional information had been collected about Piotr Palowski and his truncated visit to Ireland.

Lyons had spoken at length to an Inspector Kowalski about Piotr. The inspector had looked him up in their police database and had also consulted his colleagues. Piotr Palowski was aged twenty-seven. He was unmarried and lived with his parents in an apartment close to the centre of Krakow. He was one of four grown up children and had two sisters, Lisa and Anna, and a brother Jakub. He had no police record and worked in a local insurance company. He had a driving license and a passport, and up to recently owned a twelve-year-old VW Golf. The family was described as middle class, his father had recently retired from the same insurance company that Piotr now worked for. Piotr's mother was still working as an administrator in the Civil Service.

"The joys of the old communist system," Hays said on hearing the fulsome descriptions provided by the police in Krakow.

The car he had hired from Hertz was in a repair shop on the Airside Business Park, just up the road from the Hertz offices in Swords. Gardaí had been dispatched to secure the vehicle and take it in for forensic examination.

Hays had spent quite a while on the phone to the superintendent who was pleased to hear of the new lead, but not a bit pleased to hear of the Polish man's departure back to his homeland.

"Maureen, get back onto Inspector Kowalski and ask him if he would facilitate two Irish police questioning this Piotr guy in Krakow, with the supervision of the Krakow police of course. If he sounds positive then go home and pack your toothbrush," Hays said.

Chapter Ten

Sunday, 3:00 pm

The Ryanair Boeing 737 touched down at John Paul II International Airport in Krakow with a satisfying thud, followed by screeching from the engines as the pilot used reverse thrust to bring the plane to taxiing speed.

Krakow was already cold, but not as yet in the grip of the full Polish winter. Outside the doors leading from baggage claim to arrivals, a man with a completely shaved head stood with a piece of white cardboard bearing the four letters HAYS written freehand in black marker. He was dressed in some sort of black combat suit, with a short jacket and black pants, although there were no obvious signs that he was carrying any weapons.

He introduced himself and showed the two Irish detectives to a waiting Skoda parked quite illegally on a yellow hatched area directly outside the terminal. It was an unmarked police car, but very obviously so, with its multiple radio aerials and other equipment scattered around the dashboard inside.

Their unnamed escort drove them briskly to the centre of town, pointing out some of the major landmarks of the city on the way.

The two detectives were booked into the Radisson Blu and were surprised at the very modest rate for two rooms in a five-star hotel. It certainly lived well up to its rating, with a very simple but elegant reception area, and an inviting bar.

They were allocated rooms 220 and 221, a pair of rooms opposite each other on the second floor. Hays carried the two small cabin bags that they had brought with them to their rooms.

"Let's meet in half an hour or so downstairs. We can plan our strategy for tomorrow," he said.

"Good idea," Lyons replied, letting herself in.

When Maureen came down about forty minutes later, Hays had ordered her a gin and tonic and was half way through his first ever Polish beer.

"Thanks, Boss," she said, sitting down opposite Hays, a small piano black table between them.

"Just what the doctor ordered," she said, holding up her glass, and taking a good swig of the cold liquid.

"So, we have a meeting with Inspector Kowalski at nine-thirty tomorrow. He seems quite amenable to letting us interview Palowski. I'm not sure how it will work though. Do you think he'll bring him in to the station?" Hays asked.

"I'm not sure how it works out here. It would be good if they got him in. Do you think we need to prepare a list of questions?" she asked.

"No, I don't think so. We're pretty good together and I'd prefer just to go with the flow. You OK with that?"

"Yeah, sure. It's pretty obvious what we need to get from him in any case," Lyons said.

"A full confession to murdering his sister would be a good start!"

They had another drink, and then went out for a walk around the city. It was cold, but not unbearable, and the city had some very fine buildings and a surprising amount of green open space. They left the hotel and headed east across the squares of Krakow towards the Planty Park. They passed the magnificent façade of the Jagiellonian University, and on to Rynek Główny, the thirteenth century square right at the heart of the city. There was a mixture of architectures, going from the majestic seventeenth and eighteenth-century buildings, through the bland and faceless communist era blocks right up to the modern glass and grey metal offices that one sees in all modern cities these days. They pressed on to St Mary's Basilica with its twin towers, and caught the trumpet call at six o'clock, when the Basilica emitted a high pitched clarion sound, as it had done for several centuries. They finished their walk at the edge of the Westerplatte, and made their way back to the centre, passing the Romanesque Church of St Wojciech with its vast baroque dome that had stood since the eleventh century.

Later, after a good meal and a bottle of German wine, they made their way back to the hotel.

At the bedroom doors Hays said goodnight and then as she opened her door, he added, "Would you like some company tonight?"

Maureen immediately felt the butterflies in her stomach erupt. She said nothing but went into her room holding the door open for him to follow.

With the morning light, Hays was struggling to see how things between them could be normal and professional again after the night they had spent together. But Maureen seemed to sense his anxiety, and at breakfast she put her hand over his and quietly said, "What happens in Krakow stays in Krakow."

When Hays and Lyons left the hotel to head to the police station the weather had changed. They were met with a bitterly cold, thin wind that sliced down the narrow street like a blade. Neither of them had thought too much about what clothing they should bring to Poland, so they were ill-equipped for the Polish winter.

Thankfully, the police station was not very far away. It was an old nineteenth century building that stood formidably on a wide busy street.

As soon as they entered the building they were greeted by a strong institutional smell – a mixture of old wood, dust and carbolic soap. The walls were painted in pale green gloss paint, and the floor was a sort of grey mottled terrazzo, worn down at the entrance from countless feet tramping over it. It was also cracked here and there in the hallway.

Inside the door, a long dimly lit corridor stretched away with high oak doors in pairs to the left and right. The doors had small bevelled glass panes down to chest height, so you could see into the room. The first pair of doors on the left had the word "Recepja" painted in white on a blue board stuck to the front, which they took to be the reception area.

This area itself was a big bright room with a carved oak counter to the right-hand side. Two young officers, both female, sat behind the counter in smart blue shirts adorned with various gold coloured badges. The nearest officer, a brunette in her late twenties with her hair held back in a ponytail was called Hanna according to her lapel badge. She was the first to speak, but unfortunately in Polish, which of course neither Hays nor Lyons understood.

"We are here to see Inspector Kowalski," Hays said, hoping that Hanna spoke English.

"Ah, sorry, of course, you are the Irish Police. I'm sorry," Hanna said in perfect English with just the slightest hint of an accent.

"He's expecting you. If you go out to the hall," she said, gesturing with her hand to the corridor they had come from, "left and up the stairs one flight, his office is the second door on the left."

Hays knocked on the solid oak door. It was opened by a large man in his fifties with thinning dark hair and a ruddy face. He must have been at least six foot three in height, and while not particularly overweight, he was bulky, with broad shoulders and steely grey eyes. He wore a drab suit that had frankly seen better days, and a dark shirt with a navy-blue tie.

"Welcome," he boomed, "come in, sit down, you must be frozen. I hope you had a pleasant night at the Radisson Blu. I hear it's quite good."

Kowalski ushered the detectives to two well-worn office chairs in front of his desk.

"Coffee?" he asked.

"Yes please," they replied in unison.

Kowalski sat behind his desk and barked some instructions into the old, pale grey rotary dial telephone, presumably ordering the coffee.

"Well, I believe we have a person of interest here in Krakow for you," he said, shuffling some papers that appeared, from what Hays could decipher reading upside down, were relevant to Piotr Palowski.

Kowalski went on, "I have done a bit of snooping around on Mr Palowski. There's not a lot. He comes from a family of four children and their parents here in Krakow. His father is retired – used to be in insurance. Piotr followed his father into the same company. He has two sisters, Lisa and Anna, and a brother Jakub. Both parents are still alive, and Piotr lives with them in an apartment quite close to the centre," Kowalski said. "What's your interest in this man?"

Lyons gave an outline of the events concerning the death of Lisa Palowski in the West of Ireland and told Kowalski of Piotr's premature return to Poland the day after she had been found dead.

"We'd like to interview him, if that's possible?" Hays said.

"Do you think he killed his sister?" Kowalski asked.

"It's certainly a possibility. But we are keeping an open mind for now. We don't even know what they were doing fifty miles – sorry, seventy kilometres – from her flat out in an unpopulated area in dreadful weather," Hays said.

"Right, well I'll have him picked up at once, and you can interview him with one of my officers as soon as he gets here," he said, reaching again for the telephone.

* * *

Hays and Lyons were shown to a small room further down the corridor. It was bright but sparsely furnished with just a desk and two chairs, a phone and some plastic cups and a bottle of spring water. The most important piece of equipment in the room was an old cast iron central heating radiator which was giving off a huge amount of heat, making the room seem almost cosy, despite its barren appearance.

They had brought Kowalski's file on Piotr that he had given them. Much of it was in Polish, but there was sufficient in English to allow them to go through it.

Piotr was the eldest of the four Palowski children. There was a face picture of him in the file, presumably taken for his passport. He had short, curly fair hair, and an oval face with stark pale blue eyes and a full mouth.

The file had all sorts of details about the man. His school, his work, where he had been on holidays for the last five years, his salary and details of the company he worked for, along with all sorts of reference numbers relating to him. It also had a sheet outlining his medical history, showing that he had broken one of his arms on a skiing holiday a few years ago.

The Irish detectives were amazed at how much information the file contained. It was much more than they were allowed to see on any individual back home.

"Any thoughts?" Hays asked Lyons.

"Not a lot. I'm impressed with all the information they can pull up. And while we're at it, did you notice how Kowalski knew where we were staying even though we didn't tell him?" Lyons added.

"The driver from the airport probably told him. But we were also followed when we went walk-about yesterday afternoon. There were two of them, a man and a woman, and they stuck with us all the way round. I'm surprised you didn't spot them."

"Shit – I missed that. Some detective I am! But I wasn't looking for anything. I guess we're just not used to that level of scrutiny."

"That's why there are two of us. And you're a damn fine detective Maureen, one of the best I've worked with."

"Thanks, but that's pretty basic."

"The Poles haven't lost all their techniques from the Communist era it seems. I wonder what they'll use to pull in Piotr," Hays said.

"Probably ask him if he has a license for those eyes," Lyons said smiling.

"Oh, I see. Fancy him, do you?"

"Let's see if he's a murderer first, then I'll tell you," she replied.

Kowalski knocked on the door and came into the room.

"We have him downstairs. He wasn't too happy to be lifted from work. I want to leave him for a few minutes before we talk to him though. Let him contemplate his situation," Kowalski said. "What did you learn from the file?"

"Not a whole lot, though it's very thorough. Sergeant Lyons thinks he has nice eyes!" Hays said.

"Hmph," grunted Kowalski. "I have a few calls to make. Can we meet downstairs in say twenty minutes?" he said. "He's in room A4, and the guards will let you through. You can get more coffee at the front desk if you need it."

It was nearly half past eleven when the three detectives entered room A4 to find Piotr Palowski sitting alone at the small table in the room looking nervous. He was even better looking than his passport photo portrayed, but there was a vacuousness about him that no paper picture could ever convey.

Kowalski introduced the two Irish detectives and signalled to them that they should take over.

"Mr Palowski, as you know by now, your sister Lisa was found dead in the West of Ireland last Tuesday. We are investigating her death, and we have come here to question you as you were in the area at the time," Hays began.

"I want you to tell us from the beginning, why you travelled to Ireland, and then everything that happened from the time you arrived until you left again on Wednesday."

"I haven't done anything wrong. She was my sister, and I loved her," Palowski blurted out.

"That's not what we asked you, Mr Palowski. Now you need to answer our questions, or you will be here for a very long time," Lyons said.

"OK, OK. I came across Lisa's web page one day at work when I put her name into Google. It was disgusting. How could she do that? We are a good family. My parents think she is in Ireland studying, and there she was, selling her body. I couldn't believe it at first. It was horrible."

"So, I decided to go there and confront her, get her to stop. I called her and said I was coming over for a few days holiday, and could we go around and see the place which I heard was very beautiful. I told her I would hire a car," he said.

"So, you arrived in Dublin on the Monday, and hired a car?" Lyons confirmed.

"Yes and drove to Galway on your fabulous wide road with no traffic," he smiled.

"When did you meet up with Lisa?" Lyons went on.

"Tuesday. She told me to call her after four in the afternoon. She had things to do until then. I stopped by her apartment and she came out soon after four. She wanted to go for a drive even though it was starting to get very grey and dark. She said that it was always like that in Galway. She had heard that Clifden was nice, and asked if we could go there. We drove out in that direction," Palowski said.

"How did you know how to get there?" Lyons asked.

"I have Google Maps on my phone," Piotr replied.

"Go on then, you drove out to Clifden," Hays prompted.

"No, we drove out in that direction, but we started arguing. I started to ask her about what she was doing – you know, the page on the internet. I told her if our parents found out it would kill them, and anyway it was disgusting – she was a perfectly respectable girl in Poland with good prospects. She didn't need to do that." He was getting animated now as he remembered the row with his sister. His cheeks were beginning to colour, and a fire had come into his steely blue eyes.

"Go on," prompted Lyons.

"We got to a place, a town, with a narrow bridge and sharp bends across a river. The town name began with 'O', but I couldn't pronounce the name, and we were shouting at each other. It was horrible, so I turned the car around and drove back to the city in silence and left her at the door of her apartment," Palowski said.

"What time was this?" Hays asked.

"I'm not sure. Probably around six, I would guess, maybe six-thirty."

"What did you do then?" Hays asked.

"I went back to my hotel. I was very upset. Things had not gone the way I had hoped. I thought she would see reason, see what harm she could be doing to our family, but I had failed to persuade her. I had some food in my room, and then decided to change my flight and go back to Krakow. I logged on and changed my flight to Wednesday," he said.

Hays looked at Lyons and decided to end the interview for the time being. They would be able to check out parts of his story to see if he was telling the truth.

Outside the room Hays asked Lyons what he thought of Palowski's story.

"I think it's bullshit, but right now we can't prove it. How could she have got from Oughterard to Ballyconneely unless he drove her?" Lyons said.

They asked Kowalski how long he could keep the man in custody.

"As long as you like, but sometimes it's better to let them go, but watch them. He will think he has got away with it, and maybe slip up."

"I agree," said Lyons, "anyway it will take us some time to check with the hotel and see if he's telling the truth."

"I'll release him then but don't worry, we have his passport, and he will be watched carefully until you need him again," the Polish officer declared. They had no doubt that he would!

"Thanks. Can we get an office with an international phone for the afternoon please?" Hays asked.

"Sure. You can use my office. I have to go to one of the other stations for a meeting. Will you be here tomorrow?"

"Yes, though that will be our last day. The Irish taxpayer won't fund us for longer than a couple of days."

* * *

Hays and Lyons settled into Kowalski's office with a sandwich apiece, and two large cardboard cups of strong coffee.

Lyons got on the phone to Galway and spoke to Eamon Flynn. After a few jokes about foreign holidays, they got down to business.

Lyons asked him to check with Jury's to see if Palowski had ordered food in his room last Tuesday evening. She asked him to check if it was a single meal, and more importantly, what time it was served. She then asked him to get onto the car hire company and find out exactly how many kilometres Palowski had clocked up during the hire period. She also asked Flynn to confirm the round-trip distance between Jury's Inn in Galway and both Ballyconneely and Oughterard. Finally, she asked him to get back on to Ryanair to confirm the time that Palowski had changed his flight. Flynn said he would get John O'Connor to help him, and then asked to speak to Mick Hays.

Flynn told Hays that Lisa Palowski's phone company had been back in touch. They had managed to identify another number that had called Lisa in the days before her death from her phone. It was made from a pay-as-you-go customer, but he had topped up using a credit card, and they had been able to trace him through that.

Hays told Flynn to track the man down and get him in for questioning.

Flynn reported that there was no word back yet on the detailed forensics from Lisa's apartment. Flynn said the lab was having a hell of a time separating out all the DNA from her bed sheets and waste paper bin. Lisa had been a busy girl.

Hays reminded Flynn to get Jim Dolan to call on the Lake Guest House, and check up on Ciara O'Sullivan's story about the curtains, and more particularly, to see if there was a passenger in the car when she called.

By five o'clock Krakow time Flynn was back onto Hays. Hays put his mobile on speaker, so Lyons could join in the conversation as well.

"Well first, Palowski did have a meal in his room in Galway on Tuesday. He had a burger and a bottle of Heineken, and it was delivered at ten minutes past ten according to the night kitchen staff that run room service up to midnight when the main kitchens are closed. Then there's the hired car. If Palowski had driven to Oughterard and turned back, then adding the return trip to Dublin Airport, and a few kilometres for running around, there would be around six hundred kilometres covered in all. But Hertz confirmed that the car had actually done seven hundred and twenty kilometres, so there's an extra one hundred and twenty to account for. And yes, you guessed it, that's just about the exact round trip distance that would have got him out to Ballyconneely via Roundstone and back," Flynn reported.

"That's great work Eamon, well done. Is there anything on Lisa's other mysterious caller yet?"

"Seems that he's a travelling salesman for a paint company in Dublin, out on the Ballymount estate. He has several speeding tickets picked up on the N6. Looks like he comes to Galway once a fortnight on Tuesdays and stays overnight. The Dublin boys are getting him in for a chat. When will you two holidaymakers be back, Boss?" Flynn asked.

"Very funny. We'll leave tomorrow afternoon, but I want another hour or two with the brother before we go anywhere. He's been telling us porkies," Hays said.

"Oh, and there's one other thing, Boss. The hotel says that Palowski's hire car re-entered their car park at nine-twelve pm on Tuesday. They issue tickets at a barrier that residents get stamped at the hotel reception. It seems they don't own the car park, or it's operated by someone else at least. Their system keeps a record and has CCTV at the entrance, so they are quite positive about the time."

"Ah that's really good work, Eamon. We'll make a real detective out of you yet! Thanks again."

When the call was over, the two detectives used the blackboard in Kowalski's office to build a timeline of Piotr Palowski's movements on the Tuesday.

"Two things are clear," Lyons said. "He obviously drove out well past Oughterard with the girl in the car, according to the mileage and the time that he got back to his hotel."

"And the other?" Hays asked.

"He's lying through his teeth!"

* * *

Kowalski hadn't returned when the two detectives left the police station and walked back through the narrow wind-swept streets to their hotel. It hadn't warmed up any, so when they got in they went straight to the bar and had a large brandy apiece to warm them through.

On the way to the rooms Maureen said that she needed a shower before going out to eat. She got to her door, opened it with the plastic key card and turned to Hays saying, "I need some company," and held the door open for him.

Chapter Eleven

The weather had warmed up a bit overnight, but the cold had given way to a steady and persistent downpour. They borrowed large colourful umbrellas from the hotel, so by the time they got to the police station, only their feet and the last few inches of their trouser legs were soaking wet.

They met Kowalski going into the building. He apologised for the weather, but Lyons assured him that it rained just the same in Galway, and they were both well used to it.

They brought the Polish inspector up to date with the information that they had received from Galway the previous afternoon.

"He's not telling us the truth, Inspector, so we need to get him in again and give him a grilling," Lyons said.

"Hmm, OK. You are right, and if I can suggest, maybe one of our less polite interrogators might be helpful to you?" Kowalski said.

They agreed, not quite knowing how impolite Polish 'interrogators' might be, but they both felt that as there was not much time left, they could do with some help with the man.

* * *

Piotr Palowski was disgruntled at being dragged away from his work two days in a row. In the small stuffy interrogation room, the two Irish detectives were joined by Inspector Kurt Nowak. Nowak was burly, at about six foot two, and weighed in at something over two hundred and forty pounds. He looked quite menacing with his head completely shaved and two days of stubble on his face. A dark tattoo all up along his left forearm completed the picture. He was dressed in black jeans, and a black collarless T-shirt with the word 'Policja' in white letters front and back. His hands were like small hams, and on two of his thick fingers he wore heavy gold rings that almost looked like knuckle dusters.

They had all agreed to let Nowak lead the questioning, although it was made clear that Hays and Lyons were free to join in at any time. They had also agreed to conduct the interview in English throughout. Lyons had her trusty notebook out to record any interesting points that cropped up. Polish police didn't believe in taped interviews.

"Now Piotr, you know why you are here today, I'm sure," Nowak started in a very soft voice.

"No, I don't. I told these two everything yesterday. This is a waste of time," he grumbled.

Nowak said nothing and waited for a full thirty seconds, then suddenly without warning slapped his palm down hard on the table and shouted into Palowski's face, "You little shit. You told them a pack of lies. You expect us to believe your crap? Now listen carefully," softening his voice again, "in about ten minutes I'm going to charge you with the murder of your sister Lisa, and then my friend, you and I are going down to the cells for a little one-on-one." Nowak smiled at the thought of it, and cracked his knuckles loudly. Then, putting his face about twenty centimetres from the lad, he roared, "Tell the fucking truth."

"OK, OK. Jesus, take it easy," Palowski said. You could see that Nowak's threat had got to him. Lyons wasn't totally comfortable with the process but thought to herself, "when in Rome …"

Palowski went on, "What I told you yesterday was mostly the truth. I did collect Lisa from her apartment at around four o'clock, and we did drive out towards the west. We also had a row. But we drove out well beyond the town with the 'O' name. It was getting dark, and the weather was closing in. We were shouting at each other – it was horrible. At one point her mobile phone rang, and when she went to answer it, I lost my temper and grabbed it from her and threw it out of the window into the hedge. She was furious. She demanded that I stop the car and go and look for the phone, but I wouldn't stop. We were out in the wilderness then. The rain was lashing down, and it was windy too. She wouldn't stop shouting at me calling me 'kutas' (prick) and 'dran' (bastard) and shouting 'kurwa, kurwa'. I never heard her talk like that," he reflected.

"After I threw her phone out, she got worse. She went mad. Then we were passing a narrow point on the road, I think it might have been a little bridge. She grabbed the steering wheel, and the car slewed to the left and hit the wall.

"I backed up the car a bit. It wasn't badly damaged, just a little bashed, and a few stones had come loose from the wall. She got a fright though. She got out to look at the damage. I was feeling so shit about her and everything that I locked the doors, turned the car around and drove away," said Piotr starting to sob quietly.

"She was banging on the driver's window, shouting at me 'let me in, let me in' but I didn't, I just drove back the way we had come, I was so angry," he sobbed.

"But she was alive when I left her, I swear," he went on.

Lyons cut in, "So let's get this straight. You put your sister out of the car on a filthy October night in the lashing rain in the middle of nowhere, and just drove away?"

"Yes, I was so mad with her. I know I shouldn't have, but I thought it would teach her a lesson," he broke down again. "The last time I saw my beautiful sister she was banging on the car window. My God, it's awful, but I didn't kill her," he said, burying his face in his hands.

"OK, we need you to write all this down and sign a statement. Then we will see where we go from here, but if you're still lying I can tell you it will go very badly for you, you have my personal word on that!" Nowak said.

Back in Kowalski's office, they started to bring the inspector up to date.

"No need. I heard it all. The room has a listening device," he smiled.

"What do you make of it?" asked Lyons.

"Nowak is a very experienced interrogator. It was his job since well before the end of communism, and he has questioned hundreds of people who have done much worse than kill an escort girl. He says he thinks the little shit could be telling the truth. He's not certain, but it's definitely a possibility. Unfortunately, we can't use Nowak's full range of talents on the boy these days – too many do-gooders watching us."

"Do you think we could get him back to Ireland? I'd like to do a reconstruction of his story with him, and see how it stacks up," Hays asked.

"That could be tricky. He would have to go voluntarily. Unless you want to try and extradite him, but that could take months, maybe longer, and quite possibly would not succeed. I'll get Nowak to have another word with him in private, and maybe he will volunteer to travel to Ireland. Let's see," Kowalski said.

"We have to get back to Ireland today. Can you send on Piotr's DNA and fingerprints?" Lyons said, handing her Garda business card to Kowalski.

"And how can we be sure he won't flee the country?" Hays added.

"Don't worry about that. We'll keep his passport and a close eye on him. He won't get far if he does run. One of our men lives in the same block as he does, so we'll know his every move."

The two Irish detectives had no doubt, given what they had witnessed so far, that Piotr Palowski would be closely monitored by the Polish police. Hays and Lyons thanked Kowalski for all his help and support over the two days.

"Well, we are all Europeans now, eh? But just one thing. Next time you come to Krakow, save the Irish taxpayer some money and just book one room." He winked at Maureen and smiled.

* * *

As luck would have it, it wasn't Gerry Byrne's week for a trip to Galway. The two detectives from Store Street Garda Station in Dublin's city centre found his two-year-old Mondeo in the driveway of his house in a neat but modest estate of semi-detached houses in Templeogue. The houses were packed tightly together allowing for just a small patch of grass to the front alongside the brick driveway. Byrne's grass was well kept, and a very narrow border of flowers had been planted against the fence that divided his plot from next door.

The man that opened the door was your archetypal salesman in his mid-forties. He wore a shiny grey suit with a cheap striped tie and well-worn brown shoes. He was a bit overweight and ruddy about the face, probably from too many pints drunk in too many hotel bars up and down the country. The house showed evidence of kids, with cheap plastic toys scattered in the hallway, and family noises coming from deep within.

The Store Street detectives had no difficulty getting Byrne to go with them once Galway was mentioned. He was keen to get out of earshot of his wife and told her the Gardaí were looking for some information about one of his customers.

When they got back to Store Street, Byrne was shown to an interview room and asked to wait. The two detectives returned a few minutes later with three plastic cups and a litre bottle of cold water.

"Mr Byrne, we are making enquiries into the sudden death of a girl from Galway, a Miss Lisa Palowski."

Byrne looked back at them blankly.

"Do you know this woman?"

"No, I don't think so, should I?"

"Well yes you should," the younger detective said. "You spend an hour in her bed every time you visit Galway on every second Tuesday, so we just thought her name might ring a slight bell with you."

The colour drained from Byrne's face.

"Now look here," he protested, "I'm a respectable married man. You have no right to make those sorts of accusations."

The older detective leaned forward across the table. "Look Gerry, let's cut the crap. We have your mobile number on her phone. We have your messages to her, and we have you in her diary every second Tuesday, regular as clockwork, so don't piss us about."

Byrne thought for a moment, sighed and said, "My wife doesn't have to know about this, does she? She'd kick me out, you know."

"Perhaps, perhaps not. See, thing is, Gerry, Lisa's been murdered. Last Tuesday in fact. Just about the time you were seeing her. So, we may have a bit of a problem keeping this to ourselves."

"Murdered! Good God that's awful," he said. "I never," Byrne gasped, "yes, yes I was supposed to see her at six as usual, but when I got to her apartment, there was no reply at the door. I tried calling her mobile, but it went through to voicemail. I never saw her on Tuesday. Honest."

"What did you do then? Go back to your hotel and watch porn on your laptop?" sneered the detective.

"We'll need your other mobile."

"What do you mean, what are you talking about?" Gerry Byrne said.

"The one you used to call Lisa. We'll see if the mobile operator can place the call you made outside her apartment, then we'll see where we go from there. Oh, and if you have any other ladies that you call on regularly in any other towns around the country, now would be a good time to tell us, Gerry."

"That phone is in the boot of the car, back at the house. And as for other ladies, there is a girl in Cork that I visit sometimes. I do the Cork to Limerick run the other week when I'm not in Galway," Byrne admitted.

"Well I'd give Corky a miss from now on, Gerry, if I were you. It's only going to lead you into trouble, that sort of thing, if it hasn't already."

Byrne was very subdued as they drove him back to his family home.

When they got back to his house, he located the pay-as-you-go mobile in a hidden compartment in the boot of his car and handed it to the detective.

His wife appeared at the door.

"Hi love. It's all fine, all cleared up now. What's for tea? I'm starving," he said as he made his way towards his front door.

"Prick," the two detectives said in unison.

Chapter Twelve

Wednesday, 8:30 am

The team assembled in the incident room, keen to find out all the details about the visit to Krakow.

They had forensic reports back on James McMahon's car which confirmed the traces he predicted that they would find in the front passenger seat. No other traces of the girl, or indeed anything of interest had been found in it, so they had returned the car to him the previous evening, telling him again not to leave town.

Jim Dolan had called to the woman that ran the Lake Guest House, and she had confirmed that Ciara did not have a passenger when she called to collect the curtains at the house. She was positive about this, as she had walked out to the car with Ciara, despite the terrible weather, to see her off, and she said that O'Sullivan was definitely the only person in the car.

By nine o'clock, everyone was up to date. Store Street had emailed through the details of Gerry Byrne's phone, and John O'Connor had been tasked with contacting

Meteor to establish where the phone was when Byrne had called Lisa's phone at around six on the evening she had been killed.

Lyons and Hays withdrew to his office.

"The Super wants an update from me later on. I thought we might just have a recap on where we think we are before I brief him. Then maybe you could do up a two-page report to try to keep him at bay, not to mention the Dublin mob," said Hays.

"Yes, sure. Well let's see exactly what we have so far. As I see it there are only two likely suspects at this stage. There's the brother – he has to be number one on the list. His story about abandoning her like that just doesn't seem likely to me. And then there's McMahon. She could have been blackmailing him, or trying to, and his alibi stinks, in fact he doesn't have one. Mind you, from what we have heard, she doesn't seem like the type of girl to put herself at risk to that extent. She must have realised that McMahon was a powerful man, and you don't mess around with men like that and expect to get away scot-free," Lyons said.

"Well she didn't, did she? Get away scot-free I mean," Hays replied.

"Bear with me for a minute," Hays went on. "Let's just say the brother is telling the truth. Unlikely as it seems, he dumps his sister out of the car on a wild wet night, miles from anywhere. Jesus, even as I'm saying this it sounds nuts. Anyway, how does she get herself killed if he left her in good health?"

"Well let's look at that for a moment. Maybe someone comes along, sees the lady in the red coat walking along the road in the rain, clearly distressed, and fancies his chances. Takes her into his car – she would have been very grateful – tries it on, but she's not having any, they have a row, and he whacks her," Lyons said.

"It's just about possible I suppose but sounds about as likely as the brother's story if you ask me. Maybe we should let Nowak have his one-on-one with Palowski after all," Hays said.

"What about Ciara O'Sullivan?" Lyons asked.

"I can't see it to be honest. She seemingly didn't have Lisa in her car when she called to collect the curtains, and there's no damage to her vehicle, so it wasn't her that hit the bridge. OK, so she wasn't totally up-front with us about knowing the girl initially, but that could just have been shock. We'll keep her in mind, but I don't think so, unless we're missing something vital," he said.

"The more I think of it, the more I'm convinced that the answer lies out there, at the scene. I want every house between Roundstone and Ballyconneely knocked up, and the occupants interviewed. There won't be too many at home at this time of the year, most of those houses are holiday cottages. I want every pub in Clifden spoken to as well. We're looking for anyone who came in around nine o'clock looking like a drowned rat in an agitated state," Hays said.

"Jesus, Mulholland will love you," Lyons responded, rolling her eyes to heaven.

"I don't want him anywhere near it. Sure, we'll tell him what's going on, but get Flynn onto it. Get him to hook up again with Jim Dolan from Clifden. And I want progress reports every four hours with lists of the properties visited, who was at home, what they said and what they were doing that night. Oh, and can you produce some bullshit for upstairs – you know, steady progress being made, definite leads being followed, you know the kind of thing?"

Lyons got up to leave and was just at the door when Hays said, "Oh, and Maureen, I enjoyed our trip to Krakow – a lot."

She turned and smiled. "What happens in Krakow…" and left the room.

* * *

Flynn had taken the news of his departure to Roundstone and beyond quite well. He knew Garda Jim Dolan from some previous cases that they had worked together, and the two got on grand, being much the same age. Flynn had booked two nights at Vaughan's Hotel in Roundstone, and they had arranged to meet there at five o'clock.

They would start their investigations in the pubs of Roundstone, as directed, and then head out tomorrow along the old bog road to see if they could get any information from the locals.

Roundstone was virtually deserted as Flynn arrived just before five. It wasn't actually raining, but the roads were wet, and there was a stiff breeze whistling down the main street making it feel a good deal colder than the thermometer would have indicated. He was glad to get indoors where the hotel had a warm turf fire burning in the lobby, providing a warm welcome. He was just checking in when Dolan arrived as well. The hotel was glad to have them at this time of year, and invited them to dine in that evening, offering a special price for the four-course dinner which the two gladly accepted.

After a very enjoyable dinner which consisted of a delicious home-made chowder with proper stock and local fish, a beautifully tender roast lamb main course, all rounded off with an Irish Coffee cheesecake the like of which you wouldn't get in the best Dublin restaurants, the two mingled with the locals in the bar. They didn't declare their profession, but gently probed for any smidgen of information they could extract. It wasn't difficult to get the locals going on the story. It was the most exciting thing that had happened in these parts since the filming of The Quiet Man many years ago, and with very little prompting, the occupants of the hotel bar were chattering away advancing various theories about how the girl had met her demise. All were convinced that it was a stranger from the city that was responsible. Lisa had been dubbed "The Galway Hooker" – a reference to the particular kind of sailing boat that was popular in and around the area.

The most popular theory about what had happened was that she had been hit by a driver who had been drinking, and therefore fled the scene, probably not even realising the damage that had been done to the girl. The weather was blamed for the would-be driver's carelessness. The two Gardaí made mental notes of all of this, and filed them away carefully, thinking that if that were the case, the driver would inevitably have turned up in Clifden before nine o'clock on the night in question. However, with no CCTV anywhere, it would be difficult to trace him or her without someone coming forward to volunteer information.

Flynn and Dolan moved out from the hotel to one or two of the nearby pubs to expand their investigation. King's and O'Dowd's were always popular, but on this late autumn night, there were very few in, and by that time in any case the word had spread that there were two Gardaí from Galway snooping around, so information became even less readily available. There was mention of one or two mountainy men who lived in small remote cottages near the scene, and Flynn made a note of the names with the intention of paying them a visit the following day, but he didn't hold out much hope.

* * *

Hays arrived early as usual on Thursday. The desk sergeant handed him a small sheaf of messages as he passed by. When he got to his desk, he saw that one of the messages was from Inspector Kowalski in Krakow.

The message simply read, "Please call me."

Kowalski answered the phone as soon as it rang, and after a brief exchange of pleasantries went on to say, "You remember Inspector Nowak, I presume?"

Hays confirmed that he did indeed remember the man.

"Well Nowak had another conversation with Piotr Palowski after you left. Palowski has now agreed to travel to Ireland in an effort to clear his name," Kowalski reported.

"Excellent. That's good work, thank you, and pass on our thanks to Nowak as well," Hays said.

"That's no problem, I'm sure Nowak enjoyed getting the lad's agreement – apparently it didn't take very long."

"What are the arrangements then?" Hays asked.

"We will put him on the Ryanair flight to Dublin this afternoon. We will take him to the airport and deliver him to the steps of the aircraft, and you can arrange to have him met on arrival," Kowalski said.

"Very good. Will he be handcuffed?"

"Not for the flight itself. It's not as if he can get out of the plane once the door is closed. We will wait until we see the plane safely in the air. You might consider meeting him as he gets off the plane in Dublin. Can you get a car out to the aircraft?"

"Oh yes, that won't be a problem. And what about the cost of the ticket? I feel we need to reimburse you for that at least."

"There is no need. Ryanair were most accommodating in that regard. Their flight was actually fully booked, but they somehow managed to make room for him, and they insisted that there would be no charge 'in the interests of good relations with the Polish authorities' as they put it."

"Well that's terrific. Thank you very much, your co-operation is greatly appreciated," Hays said.

"You're welcome," Kowalski said, "you never know when we may need to call on you some day. There are a lot of our citizens in Ireland now, and I'm sure they are not all perfectly behaved."

"Anytime, Inspector. I'll let you know how we get on with him," Hays said and finished the call.

* * *

Lyons arrived into the station at just before nine, and Hays brought her up to date on the Palowski position.

"Get onto the Park and ask them to pick him up from the steps of the plane and drive him here directly. I suggest they handcuff him for the journey, more for effect than anything, but I don't want him jumping out of the car in Athlone or something and causing us more trouble."

"Good idea," she agreed, "I'm not sure what time the flight gets in, but he should be here by eleven or twelve tonight in any event."

"Right. When he gets here, make sure Flannery feeds him and puts him in a cell. He should be feeling right sorry for himself by the morning."

"What are you up to today?" Lyons asked.

"I'm going to see if I can put a bomb under the lab boys. We need the DNA results from her flat. We need to move this whole thing along a bit more quickly. Can you call the two tourists out in Roundstone and see what they have for us? That's if they're out of bed yet!"

Just as Maureen was getting up to leave, Hays said, "Fancy another trip away sometime soon?"

"I'm not sure I could stand the excitement," she smiled and making sure there was no one watching, leaned across the desk to plant a warm soft kiss on his lips.

Chapter Thirteen

Thursday, 10:00 am

It was a cool, breezy but fine day in Roundstone when the two Gardaí awoke and went down to a hearty 'full Irish' in the dining room of Vaughan's Hotel. After they got the call from Lyons, Flynn and O'Connor set out along the old bog road, heading west towards Ballyconneely. They had decided to start at the houses nearest to where the girl was found and work back from there until their quest for information ran out of steam. Then they would work forward again on towards Clifden, and hopefully arrive there just about teatime when people were starting to gather in the various pubs in the town.

As they drove along, the weak October sunshine was coming and going behind the fleeting patches of white cloud. There was a good breeze, but it stayed dry, which was a blessing. As the clouds passed in front of the sun the colours of the landscape changed beneath them from vivid purples and blues to browns and greys. Occasionally a sunbeam reflected off the surface of one of the many small lakes and struck the windscreen of the car, temporarily blinding Flynn who was driving.

By lunchtime they had called to the eight houses nearest to the bridge where Lisa had been found. Five of them were deserted – lock up and leave properties owned by the wealthier trades people from Galway and Dublin that served no purpose in the winter months, except to collect a small amount of tax for the Government. They would remain empty now till Easter next year when their owners would reappear to enjoy the solitude and beauty of their surroundings.

The other three houses were occupied by very elderly men who lived alone. The properties were generally in poor condition, with paint fading and windows rotting, but each had a large stack of hand cut turf piled against the side of the house in readiness for the winter months ahead. Only one of the occupants had a vehicle. The van, like the owner, had seen better days, and Flynn noticed that there was no NCT disk in the windscreen, and the tax disk was several months out of date. The van didn't appear to have any recent damage, just lots of rust patches blending nicely with the rust-streaked dark green paintwork.

None of the men could give any information that was helpful to the enquiry. They all said that they had heard about the accident, but that they were indoors at the time watching television as it was such a rough night.

The next house on the list belonged to Gerry and Mary Maguire. The two Gardaí knew that Maguire had been at the scene on the night the body was found, so they approached this house call slightly differently.

As they drove down the narrow rocky track with weeds growing in the middle towards the cottage, they could see a woman hanging washing out to dry in the breeze.

The house was a single storey cottage with two windows on either side of the door that was split in the middle like a stable door. It was painted dark green matching the colour of the window frames. To the side of the cottage there was a large corrugated iron shed that was pretty rusty, but still serviceable. The sliding door was open, and an old Ferguson T20 tractor painted in grey could be seen inside.

Another smaller outhouse faced the cottage and a wire mesh chicken run extended out from it with five or six brown hens clucking and scratching inside the enclosure.

As they pulled into the yard in front of the house, an energetic black and white border collie dog ran over to greet them as they emerged cautiously from their vehicle.

When the woman saw the two men getting out of the car, she stopped hanging out clothes and came over to meet them. She introduced herself as Mary Maguire, Gerry's wife.

When they had introduced themselves she said, "Why don't you come in and I'll make a cup of tea?"

Flynn and Dolan gladly accepted, and the three of them went inside, the dog being left out in the yard.

The kitchen was bigger than you would have expected from outside. There was a Stanley range built into a large open fireplace, a well-scrubbed wooden table in the middle of the flagged floor, and various appliances and cupboards around the edge of the room. The range was lighting, and the place had a warm and welcoming feel added to by the smell of recent baking.

Mary herself was around twenty-eight or thirty years old. She was slim with a good figure, although her loose blue jeans and thick knitted jumper didn't really do her justice. A brunette with shoulder length wavy hair, high cheekbones, and full red lips completed the picture. She wore no makeup, but she didn't need it, as her perfect skin and natural colouring were flattering to say the least. The two felt that Gerry Maguire had done well for himself.

"Ah sure look, it's nearly lunchtime," Mary said. "Would you two men like a sandwich to go with your cuppa?"

As Mary prepared a generous plate of cheese sandwiches and busied herself making a large pot of tea, Flynn started gently questioning the woman who seemed flattered by his interest and was quite clearly enjoying the company.

Mary and Gerry Maguire had lived in the house for eight years since they were married. They had two children, one boy and one girl aged six and seven, who were staying with their grandparents for half-term. The grandparents lived in Galway and had promised to take the children to the funfair that was still rather optimistically running in Salthill at this late time of year.

Mary was from the city as she called it – Galway of course. She had met Gerry initially when her parents had taken a rental at the caravan site at Dog's Bay when it was still operating. It had been a glorious summer that year, hot and still every day during the two weeks they had stayed there. Gerry had been doing some odd jobs on the site, putting in a few extra taps and fixing up the electrics in the somewhat basic shower and toilet block.

"I literally fell into his arms," she explained smiling. "I was coming out of the shower block in my swimming costume and tripped on my towel. Gerry saved me from a fall, and there we were. At seventeen I was mega embarrassed, but when he asked me to go out with him to a music session in Roundstone that night, I couldn't resist," she said, her eyes twinkling.

"Of course, Mum and Dad didn't approve, but here we are ten years later with two kids living in the bog!" she said, still smiling.

"What can you tell us about the night the body was found?" Flynn asked.

"God, it was awful. Gerry was very late, I was thinking something dreadful had happened to him. It was a dirty night too with strong wind and lots of rain, and when he came in he was soaking."

"He told me the story of how the poor girl had been found up at the road. He was really very upset. We didn't sleep at all that night, he was so put out," she said.

"Where had he been working till that hour?" Flynn asked.

"In Roundstone. He was doing up a holiday cottage at the far end of the town. He works really hard you know, I have no complaints in that direction," she said.

Flynn felt that it was rather an odd thing to say. Did Mary Maguire have reason to complain about her husband in some other area of their apparently blissful married life? He felt it better not to dig into that possibility for the moment, but he filed it away in case it might have some significance to the case at a later point.

Their lunch was rounded off with a good thick slice of tea brack, generously spread with butter, and more tea from a freshly made pot.

"You're not working today?" asked Dolan, getting up from the table in readiness to leave.

"No, well not in the tourist office, but there's plenty of work here as you can see. I don't go in on Thursdays at this time of year. There's no need for two of us and I'm happy to have the chance to catch up at home."

The two men thanked her profusely for her hospitality, and left feeling that their hunger had been fully satisfied, but that they still had no new information to add to the investigation, but they agreed that Mary's story seemed to confirm what Gerry had told the Gardaí on the night in question.

The rest of the day was fruitless. Again, they called on several houses that had been locked up for the winter. The few residents that they did come across knew nothing of the incident, and they both got the feeling that somehow, at some level, the natives had closed ranks. While there was no open hostility to their presence, they could sense that even if someone that they were interviewing had seen the whole thing unfold before his very eyes, he wouldn't have said a word.

* * *

Gerry Maguire came home early that day. He had finished a job he had been working on in Clifden and took a rare few hours off to get back home in time for tea. When he arrived home, he was met by Mary, who was not in the best of humour.

"We had those Gardaí here again today, nosing around. They were nice enough, but they were asking a lot of questions about you," Mary reported.

"They can ask all they like. I've nothing to hide. And I suppose you told them everything without batting an eyelid. You know sometimes, Mary, I think you're really thick," Gerry said, sneering a little.

"I'm thick is it. I'm thick – well that's a good one. Here we are living in the middle of bloody nowhere having to send the kids back to my parents for a bit of civilization, we've bugger all money. I haven't had a holiday in the eight years since I married you, and you're never even bloody well here. And you call me thick!" she said, raising her voice an octave or two.

Gerry Maguire slapped his wife hard across the face with the back of his hand sending her reeling across the room and causing her to lose her balance and fall against the sink.

"Right, that's it, you big bully. You can feck off with your tea," she said throwing his plate of eggs on the floor, "and you can sleep in the barn tonight – again. You're not coming near me, that's for sure."

* * *

The Ryanair flight from Krakow touched down at a few minutes past six, fifteen minutes ahead of schedule. The Polish police had arranged that Palowski should be taken off the flight first, and as soon as he reached the bottom of the aircraft steps he was met by two special branch Gardaí who took him, handcuffed him, and put him in the back of the unmarked Mondeo.

There was no conversation with the Polish man during the drive to Galway. Neither did they stop en route, so that it was just after nine o'clock when they delivered Palowski to Sergeant Flannery at the front desk of the Garda station in Galway.

Palowski was provided with a take-away meal from the nearest burger joint, and placed in a cell for the night, minus his belt, shoelaces and tie. Flannery checked him every hour or so, and he appeared to sleep for most of the time, perhaps pondering his fate when morning came.

Chapter Fourteen

Somehow, the newspapers had got wind of Palowski's return to Ireland. "Polish suspect returns to Galway," read the headline in the Connaught Tribune.

"Just what we don't need," said Hays to Maureen Lyons over their morning coffee in Hays' office.

"Can you get the media relations guys on to it and ask for a little space for a day or two? Promise them we'll give them any developments as they happen, but we need to be able to move around without a pack of journos up our arses," Hays said, feeling vexed that this information should have leaked out.

"Any news from the lads out West?" he asked.

"Nothing much," she said as she related the visit to Mary Maguire's house. "It's pretty deserted out there at this time of year to be honest."

"OK, let's get them back in then if there's no one coming forward."

"I want to take Palowski on a reconstruction run today. You can note down everything he says. We'll get him to drive one of the pool cars to make it realistic and go over the drive out to Ballyconneely where he supposedly dumped his sister out of the car in the rain," Hays said.

"Caution him before we go," he added.

"Did you get anything from the lab yesterday afternoon?" Lyons asked.

"Dozy buggers say it will be Monday before they have the DNA report. They say they got four different semen samples from the waste bin in her bedroom, and countless more from the sheets. They are focussing on the four samples initially. They say they should have something by Monday morning," he said.

"Any plans for the weekend?" Hays asked.

"Not yet, but I'm forever hopeful," she replied, smiling at her boss.

At ten o'clock they took Piotr Palowski out of his cell where he had spent a most uncomfortable night. He was nervous, probably envisaging some more of the Nowak treatment.

They outlined the plan, explaining that he was still under caution, and went outside to find the grey Opel Astra that they had booked out for the reconstruction.

The weather was cool and dry, but overcast, and it wouldn't be long before the south westerly wind deposited more Atlantic rain on the region.

They drove out along the N59, out past the University and on through Moycullen towards Oughterard. Palowski was silent for the most part, just occasionally commenting on some local feature as they passed by.

Lyons tried to engage the man in conversation about his sister. She asked if they had been a close family growing up. What their parents did for a living, where they had gone on holidays as children, and what kind of community they belonged to in Krakow. Palowski said that they had been a fairly happy lot, but that it had been very hard during the communist times. His father worked in insurance, and he worked hard for a small salary by European standards. His mother worked as a civil servant and had sometimes been called upon to teach in a primary school when there was a shortage of qualified teachers.

He said that when communism ended, everything changed. His father's company was privatized, and he began to earn better money – not a fortune, but enough to put some by every month when the essentials had been paid for.

Lisa had always been the clever one, getting good grades at school. She said one day she wanted to be a doctor. Not a medical doctor, a doctor of the mind. Mr Palowski had saved like crazy and borrowed from his brothers to send Lisa to Ireland to study and fulfil her dreams.

"And what did she do?" he said, thumping the steering wheel with the flat of his hand, "she pissed in his face. Kurwa!"

At Maam Cross they stopped for a coffee at Peacock's souvenir, grocery, café place that attempted to provide every one's needs at all times, and the only commercial operation for miles. They welcomed the break, and an opportunity to stretch their legs, and although the rain was threatening and the sky a heavy grey, it had held off so far.

Just after Recess, Hays instructed Palowski to take a left onto the R341 for Roundstone. Palowski slowed right down to navigate the narrow and twisty road. They passed the Angler's Rest where the road to Cashel branched off and continued on into Roundstone village. On a grey day in late October Roundstone was virtually deserted, with just the little green An Post van meandering slowly up the main street. Even the car park opposite Vaughan's hotel was almost empty.

As they drove out past Gurteen and Dog's Bay, Palowski became sullen again, and reflecting his mood, the clouds darkened and the rain began to fall. Lyons began to probe him again as they made their way slowly across the old bog road towards Ballyconneely.

"What were you and Lisa talking about at this point?" she asked.

"She had told me about what she was doing. She said it had started just as a way of making a little extra money to help her through college. She had been at a party one night and had quite a lot to drink. One of the tutors had offered her a hundred euro to sleep with him, and as she sort of liked him anyway, she said 'why not.' Before she knew it, she was making twelve hundred euro a week, but she had to give up most of her studies to make time for her 'business'."

"At one stage she even sent money home, saying that she had got some part-time work, and didn't need it. Pah – dirty, filthy money," he sneered.

Lyons couldn't help thinking that Lisa Palowski wasn't all bad. Not your typical escort girl at all. She wondered how many other students from Poland and other poorer Eastern European countries would not have done exactly the same if they were blessed with her good looks and found themselves in a faraway country.

As they approached Ballyconneely, Hays told Palowski to provide a running commentary on exactly what had happened that Tuesday night. He wanted every detail.

"We were driving just along here when Lisa's phone rang. She fished it out of her coat pocket and was going to answer it. It was clear to me that it was one of her clients. I got very angry. I grabbed the phone from her, opened my window, and threw the thing out. She screamed at me that it was the only number her clients could contact her on, and she needed it very badly. She begged me to stop to find it, but I wouldn't. I just kept driving."

"The weather was awful. The rain was blowing across the car, and I couldn't see very well. I was tearful as well, listening to my beautiful sister who had so easily become a whore," he said.

"I was shouting at her and then the car suddenly hit the edge of the wall, and of course we stopped. I didn't know what to do. I was afraid the car wouldn't go again. Lisa told me to back up a bit, and as she had a good coat, she would get out and see what the damage was. When I saw her outside in the light from the headlights, I had a flash of inspiration. I was looking at her standing there in her fancy new clothes, looking quite beautiful, her hair blowing all over her face in the wind, and I just couldn't stand it," he said.

"I reversed the car quickly across into that gateway over there, turned and drove off. She must have realised what was happening, because she came over to the car and started beating on the windows. I had locked the doors, but she started shouting 'Piotr, Piotr, what are you doing?', but I ignored her and just kept turning the car, and then I drove off into the night leaving her by the side of the road. I didn't hurt her, but I am responsible," he sobbed, burying his head in his hands.

The Astra was now stopped at the side of the road close to the wall that Palowski had hit on the night his sister died. Hays told him to turn off the engine and give him the keys, and then told Palowski to get out. Hays and Lyons got out too, and the three of them stood there in the rain. Hays got Palowski to show them exactly where he had stopped that night and to point out the gateway that he had reversed into to turn the car.

"So, you were in a rage with your sister, out here, no one around. She had provoked you, and then there was the phone call from one of her punters. I think you lost your temper completely and followed her outside, picking up a rock from the bridge that had fallen on the road, and whacked her over the head. Isn't that what actually happened, Piotr, isn't it?" Lyons demanded.

"No, no, of course not. I told you, I drove away and left her. She was fine. How do you think I feel now that she was killed out here? I have to live with that for the rest of my life. I wish it had been me that was knocked over the head, not Lisa. It's so horrible," he sobbed.

"Well she was hardly fine, now was she Piotr?" Hays cut in. "Outside, in foul weather, miles from anywhere on a strange road, being deserted by the brother that she loved and respected. No, sir, not fine at all."

"Look, why don't you tell us what really happened, Piotr?" Lyons said in a softer tone. "Get it over with. You'll feel better, and we can release Lisa's body so she can be buried – don't leave her lying on a cold slab in a mortuary. It won't be so bad. You'll probably get to serve most of your sentence in Poland anyway."

"Listen, I'm telling you, I shouldn't have left her here. I know that, and I am truly sorry for what happened to her. I will never forgive myself, and if I could turn back time, I would do things very differently. But I didn't harm her. I couldn't do that. You must believe me, you must."

* * *

"Maureen, have forensics still got Palowski's hire car?" Hays asked back at the station.

"Yes, it's in the garage covered in a tarpaulin."

"OK, get them to examine the carpet in the driver's footwell. If Palowski got out of the car to kill his sister, he will have brought some Ballyconneely gravel or sand back into the car on his shoes. Probably quite a bit, given the weather. Get anything they find on the floor analysed and compared to road grit from the scene."

When she had put the call through to the forensic lab, Maureen came back into Hays' office.

"What do we do now?"

"Not much we can do till Monday. We'll have the forensics from the car and the flat then. Let's see what that brings," he said.

"Do you think it was the brother?" she asked.

"Probably. But we're going to have a hell of a job proving it unless he confesses. Maybe we should get Inspector Nowak over to beat it out of him."

"Maybe." Lyons paused for a moment and then went on, "Listen, I have a voucher for a one-night dinner bed and breakfast for Killarney. They have rooms available for tomorrow night. Fancy it?"

"Yeah, OK, sounds like fun. Why don't I pick you up at yours at, say, ten tomorrow morning?"

"Cool. You're on," she said.

As an afterthought she said, "What do we do with Palowski?"

"Leave him downstairs. A couple of days down there living off Galway's finest fast-food may loosen his tongue a bit. We'll talk to him on Monday."

Chapter Fifteen

Lyons was at her desk when Hays arrived on Monday morning. They were both still basking in the warm afterglow of their night away in Kerry. They had enjoyed it immensely, leaving behind all the anxiety of the case and soaking up the peace and beauty of the countryside around Killarney.

Back in the real world, the duty sergeant told them that Palowski had spent a sullen weekend in the cells. The sergeant had tried to engage him in conversation, but he was having none of it, suspecting that the sergeant's friendly attitude was a ruse to get information from him to pass on to the detectives.

"Any more thoughts about the Pole?" asked Lyons.

"Let's wait for the forensic reports, and then we'll see what we can do about him. He's not going anywhere for now, that's for sure."

At nine o'clock the other two members of the team arrived. They had called to every occupied property along the old bog road, in the vicinity of the murder, and had come up with absolutely nothing. No one had seen or heard anything out of the ordinary on that Tuesday, in fact no one had seen anything at all, ordinary or otherwise.

Hays asked Flynn to go back to the garage where Palowski's car was being kept, and to hurry along the analysis of the grit from the driver's side footwell.

Soon afterwards, the detailed forensic report from Lisa's apartment came in. Hays brought Lyons into his office and handed each page to her as he finished reading it. It was the third page that caught his attention.

"Well fuck me," he exclaimed, "you're not going to believe this!"

Hays was looking at the DNA results from the waste paper basket that had been taken from beside the bed in Lisa's room. The third entry showed that Gerry Maguire's DNA had been found in a semen stained tissue, and also on the bed sheet.

Hays handed the page over.

"Christ! So nice happily married handyman Gerry was a client of Lisa's," she said, hardly believing what she had read.

"Yeah, I know. If it is him, he's one cool customer, and don't forget he has an alibi. How do you think we should play it?"

"I think we should pick him up from home with a marked squad car, blue lights and all. Bring him in here and let him sweat for a while," she said.

"Agreed. But before that I want to talk to whoever gave him that alibi in Roundstone where he was supposed to be working that night. If we can crack that open, we might just have our man," Hays said.

"Let's wait till he's home tonight before we lift him. It will be more dramatic after dark anyway, and it will give us a chance to get out there and see about this alibi."

* * *

The weather was still grey and overcast as Hays and Lyons approached Roundstone. They asked at O'Dowd's pub for directions to Geraghty's house and took the opportunity to down a delicious smoked salmon salad. Hays would have liked a nice creamy pint of Guinness to wash it down but held back so that he could fully focus on the job in hand.

They found the place where Maguire was allegedly working, up a twisty narrow single-track road behind the town. The road was tarred, but the surface had broken up in the frequent heavy rain, and their car rocked and bumped over the many potholes before they arrived at the cottage on the left of the lane with a fabulous view out over Roundstone harbour and out to sea. Jim Geraghty was painting the outside of the cottage when the two detectives drove up. He looked curiously at their car, and the two that got out of it. Geraghty was a man in his fifties dressed in a dirty grey T-shirt and badly stained blue jeans. His substantial beer-belly hung out well over his belt, and his greasy grey hair and ruddy cheeks completed the picture of a man that was none too fussy about his appearance, or indeed his general well-being.

Hays introduced them and asked if they could have a word inside the house.

They made their way into the parlour of the small cottage where work was still in train to bring the place up to an acceptable standard. There was a lot to do. The floor, although slabbed with large stone flags, was uneven, and some of them were badly cracked making the surface rough. A large open fireplace housed a trivet for a kettle or a pot, and the remains of a turf fire, now cold in the grate, gave off a smell of ashes, some of which had clearly blown around the room in the draught. On the wall to the left of the old fireplace hung a framed photograph of President John F Kennedy, but the corresponding picture on the right of the chimney, which should have been of the Pope, had been removed, leaving a black outline against the nearly white wall.

"Do you live here yourself?" Lyons asked, noting that the place had very little furniture – just a bare wooden table with a milk carton on it, and two well-worn rail backed chairs.

"Not at all," Geraghty replied gruffly, as if the detective should have known better than to ask such a daft question.

"I inherited the place last year when my father died and I'm doing it up for next summer to let it out to tourists," he said.

"Who's helping you with the work?"

"I'm doing it myself, as you can see, but I've got a few lads in for some of the specialty stuff – kitchen, electrics, plumbing."

"Who's doing the kitchen for you?" she asked.

"Yer man Maguire is giving me a hand when he has time. Feck all use he is too, I'd be better doing it myself. He's too busy, and when he does come he only does a bit, and then he's away again." Geraghty wheezed and coughed a noisy, fluid cough, as if the utterance of the long sentence had been a bit much for his fragile lungs. He went purple about the face before eventually regaining composure.

"Can you confirm that Mr Maguire was here last Tuesday week between five and nine o'clock Mr Geraghty?" Lyons continued.

"If he says he was, then he was. I don't pay much attention to the days to be honest. Why – what's he done?"

"You gave information to one of our colleagues that Gerry Maguire was definitely here working on your kitchen between those times. Can you confirm that?" Lyons went back at him, trying not to show her frustration.

"Look, Maguire comes and goes when he pleases. He asked me to say he was here if anyone was asking, so that's what I said. Now can you leave me in peace to get on with my work before the light starts to fade?" Geraghty said, getting up from the table.

Lyons decided not to push it any further. There was no point. But it was clear to both of them that Maguire's so-called alibi was useless.

They left Roundstone and headed into Clifden where they intended to set up the arrest of Gerry Maguire with Sergeant Mulholland. When they got to the Garda station Mulholland was there on his own, muddling through a pile of paperwork at a very easy pace.

Hays told Mulholland of the plan to lift Gerry Maguire later that evening and bring him to Galway. Mulholland said that Jim Dolan was off for the day, and that he had the Garda car with him, his own vehicle being out of order at the moment. Mulholland thought Dolan might be taking his elderly mother to Galway for a hospital appointment.

"Well you'd better make sure that both he and the car are back here by eight o'clock," said Hays in disbelief.

"Oh, by the way, the doc was looking for you earlier. Said he couldn't raise you on the mobile. He asked if you could give him a call," Mulholland said.

Hays called Julian Dodd's number using the landline at the station but was told that the doctor had gone out for an hour or two, and that he would call Hays back when he returned.

* * *

Julian Dodd, as good as his word, phoned Hays at Clifden Garda station as soon as he returned to his desk.

"Inspector, I wanted to call you about two things that may be of interest, though I'm not entirely sure to be honest," Dodd said.

"Firstly, I was talking to the forensic boys. There's no trace of any grit or sand in the driver's side footwell of the hire car that young Palowski was driving – nothing from out Ballyconneely way in any case. But here's a funny thing. I was doing a bit more work on the girl last week and I combed out her hair. I found some small grains of what I assumed to be sand in both her hair and her right ear. Just to be sure, I sent them off to be analysed, and guess what?" he said, continuing without a pause, "they turned out to be sawdust!"

"Sawdust!" Hays exclaimed, looking over at Lyons in surprise.

"Yes, and there's more. The analysis shows that it's a very particular kind of sawdust. The sawdust itself is from a high density MDF board, but there are particles of dark grey composite material mixed in with the sawdust, so it looks as if they have come from a kitchen worktop or some such thing," Dodd said.

"OK, Doc. Thanks for that. It could be really important. Make sure that those samples are carefully preserved for us, won't you?"

"Of course. No need to ask," Dodd said, and hung up.

Hays related the call to Maureen Lyons.

"Come on," she said, "we have time to get back to Geraghty's cottage and collect some samples of our own before Maguire is brought in. Let's go."

They drove the old bog road back to Roundstone as quickly as the undulating surface would allow without making them both sick. Back at the cottage Geraghty was just finished painting the outside of the house in the fading light and was packing up his brushes, ladder and other equipment. He was none too pleased to see the two detectives arriving back.

"What ails you this time?" he asked gruffly as the two approached him.

He reluctantly allowed them to collect some sawdust gathered from the base of the kitchen worktop, but when they asked for a small off-cut of the worktop itself he got cute and asked them for a receipt.

Lyons was well up to this kind of nonsense.

"Certainly, Mr Geraghty, that's no problem. But you'll have to accompany us to Clifden Garda station and sign a statement to the effect that these samples were taken from your kitchen. It could take a few hours. And then there's the small matter of the alibi you provided initially for Mr Maguire. You'll have to rescind that and give us a proper statement about that Tuesday. There may even be charges arising from your initial story," she said.

"Ah to hell with you both. Get out of my sight," he snarled, and he turned and continued to tidy up his painting stuff.

Maureen smiled to herself.

* * *

The Clifden squad car driven by Jim Dolan bounced down the dirt track to Gerry Maguire's house with its blue lights flashing. As Dolan pulled into the yard and stopped by Maguire's van he put on the sirens for a moment just to add a bit more drama to the occasion.

Both Gerry and Mary Maguire appeared at the door and Dolan explained that he was arresting Gerry Maguire on suspicion of the murder of Lisa Palowski, and read him his rights.

Amid much protestation and a lot of tears from Mary, Gerry was finally bundled into the back of the squad car. Dolan was now quite wound up, so he drove back up the lane aggressively, with the suspension of the old Ford bottoming on the rocky track. He had, as instructed, got the blue lights flashing. Maguire started to speak to the Garda, but Dolan told him to stay quiet. It would be better for him if he said nothing at this point, the Garda pointed out.

* * *

Hays and Lyons had returned to Galway Garda station, stopping at the forensic lab to drop off the samples taken from Geraghty's cottage.

When Maguire arrived after a hair-raising drive from Ballyconneely, he was shaken and angry at the same time.

He was shown into an interview room and given a cup of tea before being joined by Hays and Lyons.

As soon as they entered the room, Maguire started to protest his innocence.

"All I did was try to help. This is so wrong. You have no right to grab me from my home in front of my wife like that. She's distraught. I need to get home to her," he ranted on.

When he stopped for breath, Lyons got a chance to start her questioning.

"See here, Gerry, you haven't been entirely honest with us, now have you?"

"Tell us everything about you and Lisa Palowski."

"I don't know what you mean. All I know is that I stopped to see if I could help and look what it's done for me. I should have left it alone," he said, looking away to the side of the bare room as if to imply that the matter was concluded.

"But you knew the girl before you allegedly came across the scene that night, Gerry, didn't you?" Lyons pressed on.

"What are you talking about? Of course I didn't know her. That's crazy!"

"Crazy is it. Well how come we found your semen on a tissue in her bedroom then, and more of it on her bed sheets. How do you think that got there?" Lyons asked.

"That's nonsense. You're making it up. You're trying to frame me. I'm an honest working man with a lovely wife and a happy marriage," he insisted.

"Aye, Mary's a grand girl OK," Hays interjected, "makes you wonder why you'd want to spend your time screwing a hooker."

"That's bollocks. You've made a mistake. Let me out of here," he shouted.

"And then there's the matter of exactly where you were on that Tuesday before you allegedly turned up where Lisa was lying in the ditch," Lyons said.

"I told you. I was working at Jim Geraghty's cottage doing the kitchen," Maguire replied.

"Good one, Gerry. Very good," Hays said, leaning across the table to bring his face nearer to Maguire's. "It's just that Jim Geraghty won't confirm that. And what's more, he says you told him to say you were there if anyone asked."

"I'll tell you what's going to happen now, Gerry. Sergeant Lyons and I are going to take an hour or so to catch up on some paperwork. You can stay here and make your mind up to start telling the truth. Do you need something to eat?" Hays asked.

"I'm not feckin' hungry. I just need to get out of here back to Mary."

"It's not going to happen, Gerry. Not till you start being honest with us," Lyons added getting up to leave.

* * *

Back in Hays' office Lyons called the forensic lab. They had arranged for a technician to stay on to compare the fragments found on the dead girl to the samples they had collected from the floor of Geraghty's cottage. When she had finished the call, she told Hays that tests were ongoing, but there was a ninety per cent chance of a good match at this stage. If they had been able to recover more of the dust from the girl's hair, the process would be quicker.

"Ninety per cent is good enough for me," Hays said to Lyons.

* * *

They took more tea back into the interview room when they resumed their questioning of Gerry Maguire.

"Now then. Can we just go over this once again with you, Gerry?" Lyons said, putting a plastic cup of tea down in front of him.

"All right. Listen. I did go with Lisa a few times in Galway. It didn't mean anything, it was just sex. Mary seems to have gone off the whole thing lately, and well, you know, a man has needs."

He went on to describe how he met her when he was doing some electrical work at her apartment building. She had been kind to him, giving him tea and biscuits, and one thing led to another till they ended up having sex on three or four occasions. He had paid her twice, but the other two times he had done work on her flat in exchange for sex. He knew she was an escort, but he said it wasn't like that between them, it was more than just a commercial relationship. They had talked a lot too. About her life in Poland and her family. Gerry had told her a lot about himself too. About Mary, his first love, and how things had started to go wrong between them. How they bickered a lot, and how sex had become a rarity in recent times.

"When were you last with her?" Lyons asked.

"On the Monday, the day before she died. She wanted an extra socket put into the kitchen for a new coffee machine she had bought in Argos. So, I went there, and after I had fitted the new plug we made love."

It's an old story, Lyons thought to herself. The client almost falls in love with the escort, and always thinks that there's more to it from her side too. And Lisa Palowski would have been very good at cultivating those feelings in her clients. Lyons was sure if you asked James McMahon and Gerry Byrne about it, they would say that they were special to her as well – more than just a source of money. Indeed, McMahon had already told them that he did favours for her, driving her around to get her shopping. In extreme cases, the punter tries to save the girl from a life of debauchery, and usually ends up getting badly hurt. These girls instinctively know how to play their clients. How gullible some men are, she mused.

"So, what happened the following night Gerry?" Lyons asked.

"It's just as I said. I was driving home in the rain, and I came across you lot at the bridge. I couldn't believe it was Lisa. I had no idea what she was doing there or how she got there. I was very upset. It was awful. She was a very beautiful girl, you know, and here she is lying in the bog dead. It was unbelievable," he said.

"Well, Gerry, that's not really true, is it?" Hays said.

"Of course it is. It's like I said."

"Well then, Gerry, how do you explain that we found traces of sawdust in the girl's hair? Sawdust that matches the sawdust from Geraghty's cottage and that we could see clearly on your clothes when we first spoke to you at the scene?" Lyons asked.

"It must have fallen off me when I was standing there," Maguire said, thinking quickly.

"I don't think so. See, we found sawdust in Lisa's right ear too. That side of her head was down in the ditch under water. It must have got there before she fell in," Lyons said.

Maguire leaned forward, his head in his hands and began to sob. His whole body was shaking, and the tears flowed freely. After a while he confessed to what had really happened on that terrible night out on the old bog road.

He had been driving home at about eight o'clock when he saw Lisa sitting on the bridge wall, drenched from the rain, just sitting there. His mind went into overdrive. What was she doing here, so close to his home? Oh no. She had come to tell Mary about them. How he had promised to take her away from her sordid life and look after her. She was going to ruin his marriage and destroy his family. He just couldn't let that happen. He had stopped the van and got out. When Lisa saw who it was, she ran to him and threw her arms around his neck, sobbing, 'take me home' she had said, 'take me to your house, Gerry.'

She had clung to Gerry like a limpet, holding him to her tightly. She kept asking him to take her home, that they could be together now as they had wanted. Gerry's mind was racing. He saw the loss of his family, the loss of Mary, and his reputation all disappearing in front of his very eyes, and he knew he had to get rid of Lisa before someone came along the road and saw them together.

"You know I can't take you home, you silly bitch! What are you doing here anyway? Coming out here to ruin me, no doubt," he shouted at her above the noise of the wind. All she could say in reply was, "No, no, Gerry, I want you. We can be together, take me home with you."

Gerry began to lose his temper. A fierce rage grew in him fuelled by a strong desire for self-preservation and the need to get rid of this woman before some real damage was done.

He pushed her away harshly, and as she turned around with her back to him, he picked up a rock from the top of the wall and struck her hard at the back of the head. She fell to the ground, blood pouring from the wound. His temper still up, Gerry rolled her away to the side of the road and pushed her into the ditch. He knew she was dead – the light had gone from her eyes, and she had stopped breathing.

As he calmed down, he began to feel remorse for what he had just done, but again, his preservation instincts were strong, and a plan began to form in his troubled mind. There had been no one about, no one had seen what had happened, and if he was a bit crafty, he felt he could get away with the killing. He just needed to keep his head.

He drove the van back to the old abandoned caravan site at Dog's Bay. He climbed over the wall and used the old ruined toilet block to clean himself up and remove any traces of the girl from his hands and clothes. The place was ghostly on that wild night, with the wind whistling through the broken windows, and the rain lashing the tin roof. Luckily, there was water running in the old taps, and he managed a cursory wash and clean up, although there was no towel that he could use to dry himself. But by now he was calm and had decided on a plan that would see him in the clear, as long as he kept his head.

Then he drove back and stopped when he saw the Gardaí milling around at the scene, letting on that he had just come from work.

* * *

They had taken a full statement from Gerry Maguire where he had admitted the murder of Lisa Palowski out on the old bog road on that dreadful Tuesday night. He had been put back in the cells, pending a court appearance the following morning in the district court in Galway where the Gardaí expected him to be remanded in custody till a trial date could be set.

Mary Maguire had turned up at the Garda station in Galway soon after Gerry had arrived. A female Garda had been found to look after her while her husband was being processed. She was in a terrible state, claiming that her husband was a good man, and was absolutely incapable of harming another person, let alone a woman.

Hays had telephoned the superintendent to let him know of the developments. He was pleased with the outcome and congratulated both Hays and Lyons and the rest of the team for their good work in bringing the matter to a close. He told Hays to make sure that the forensics were in good shape, adding, "You know how difficult it is to get a conviction solely on the basis of a confession these days." Hays assured him that they had enough on Maguire to convict even without the confession, but that he would of course ensure that all the evidence was preserved in preparation for the trial.

"I think he'll probably plead guilty when it comes to it, to be honest," said Hays.

Back in his office, Lyons and Hays cracked open a bottle of whiskey to drink to the successful closure of what had been a very challenging case for both of them. There was no sign of O'Connor and Flynn – they would be able to celebrate tomorrow, they agreed.

"What do we do with the Polish lad?" Lyons asked. "Are we going to fly him back to Krakow?"

"Not bloody likely. This isn't Thomas Cook you know," Hays said smiling. "We'll give him fifty euro and let him go in the morning. He'll find his own way home. Oh, and remind me to call Kowalski and give him the good news. I suspect he'll want to tell the family that their son is innocent."

Chapter Sixteen

Tuesday, 10:00 am

Piotr Palowski had been released from the cells in Galway's police station shortly after eight o'clock. He had been given the fifty euro that Hays had promised, and the desk sergeant gave him directions to the bus station where he could get a coach directly to Dublin Airport. They had even looked up the times of the flights back to Krakow that day for him, and he was going to comfortably make the five o'clock Ryanair flight with time to spare.

Outside the courthouse down by the Corrib river there were several photographers and even a TV crew awaiting the arrival of Gerry Maguire. Word had got out during the night that a man had been charged with the murder of Lisa Palowski, and the reporters knew that he would be brought to court that morning to go before a judge.

The white Garda van arrived just before the hour and drove into the yard at the side of the courthouse. Maguire was escorted from the van with a grey coat covering his head, and led into the court by two Gardaí, one of whom was handcuffed to him.

The hearing lasted all of four minutes. Maguire confirmed his name and address for the court, and as there was no bail application, he was remanded to appear before the court again in two weeks' time.

Tradition has it that prisoners are taken from the courthouse by the front steps and walked around to the side yard before being loaded back into their transport and taken off to the remand centre at Castlerea Prison. As Maguire left the courthouse, again escorted by two uniformed Gardaí, photographers crowded in around him, although his face was mostly covered by the same grey coat.

In the melee, suddenly, a man with fair curly hair pushed through the crowd and faced Gerry Maguire. Maguire felt the blade pierce his skin, and the cold steel entering his torso. It went in deep, puncturing his heart, so by the time anyone realized what was happening Maguire was slipping to the ground, pumping blood out onto the cold granite steps.

Panic ensued amongst the crowd, with photographers not knowing whether to try to assist, or just to get the best photos for the evening papers. In the confusion the assailant slipped away and was gone. He dumped the knife in the river and walked off, hands thrust deep into his pockets mingling with the other pedestrians heading up town.

Hays and Lyons came out of the courthouse next and were greeted by a scene of total chaos. Maguire lay bleeding on the ground, the Garda who was handcuffed to him desperately struggling to release himself from the victim, shouting, "For heaven's sake will someone call an ambulance – he's been stabbed!"

Mary Maguire emerged behind Hays and Lyons and dashed to her husband's side, holding his head in her hands and wailing, "Gerry, Gerry, what have they done to you? Oh God, Gerry, don't leave me." The ambulance arrived, and a gap was cleared through the throng to allow the paramedics to bring through a stretcher. Maguire was unconscious, though the ambulance men had managed to stem the bleeding for the most part. He was loaded into the ambulance and given oxygen. Mary accompanied him as they set off to the Regional Hospital with sirens blaring, but by the time they arrived in front of the building, Gerry had stopped breathing. All attempts by the hospital staff to revive the man were of no use, and soon afterwards he was pronounced dead.

When Hays and Lyons got back to the station, any sense of celebration had dispersed. News had travelled back quickly, and as they walked through the building to Hays' office, various Gardaí passed them and muttered their sympathy.

"He'll either be on the train or the bus back to Dublin," Lyons said. "My guess is the bus that goes directly to the airport. I'll have them set up road blocks outside Athlone, and we can put some men on the trains just in case he decides to go that way. He can't do anything else – he has very little money, and he'll want to be getting out of here."

* * *

The phone on Hays' desk rang. When he finished the call he said to Lyons, "He was sitting in the fourth row of the airport coach, just like you said. He didn't resist. The boys in Athlone have him, and he'll be back here by teatime. I'll call Kowalski again and bring him up to date."

"Thank God that's over," Lyons said. "Now we can get back to a bit of ordinary burglary. Oh, by the way, I got some more vouchers." She smiled at her boss.

Chapter Seventeen

Superintendent Finbarr Plunkett sat on a stool at the bar in the Connemara Golf Club enjoying a pint of Guinness and a small whiskey chaser.

James McMahon stood beside him clutching a gin and tonic. It was eight o'clock at night, and the two had enjoyed a pleasant round of golf, playing in a four-ball with two other members of the club. After the golf, they had polished off a good-sized steak apiece, and were now on their after-dinner drinks.

"That was a queer business with that Maguire fellow after all, wasn't it Finbarr?" McMahon said.

"It was to be sure. I hope our fellows weren't too hard on you while all that was going on?"

"Ah not really. They had their job to do, and I'm very glad that we managed to keep it from Jennifer and the family, that would have been very difficult for me," McMahon said.

"God, it would. I had a word with Hays at the time, told him to go easy with you. I didn't say we were friends, but he knows which side his bread is buttered on all the same."

"That girl he has with him is a bit of a terrier," McMahon said.

"You can say that again. She's a damn fine detective, but a bit unpredictable, and to be honest she'd be a lot harder to rein in than Hays. That's why we keep her a sergeant – don't let her have too much power," Plunkett said, smiling.

"And what happened with the young fella that did away with Maguire anyway? It was like bloody Dodge City round here for a while. Two murders in two weeks!"

"Ah the lad was destroyed with grief and remorse. He reckoned it was his fault that his sister was killed. Could be right too, it was a damn stupid thing to do, leaving her out in the rain like that and driving off. When we let him go, he went and got a knife and decided to take his revenge for his sister's death out on the man who killed her. Almost biblical if you like," Plunkett said. "He got done for murder of course and was given twelve years with the last three suspended, but he won't serve much time here. The Polish authorities have been badgering us to let him go back to Poland to serve it out, and to be honest, with the state of our prisons, one less to look after would be a blessing. But the politicians have got hold of it now, so anything could happen."

"And what about you, James?" Plunkett went on. "That was a pretty close call for you too. Are you still seeing someone from time to time?"

"Now, Finbarr, that would be telling. But if I am, and I said 'if', then I'd be a damn sight more careful in future," McMahon replied.

"Be sure you are James. We can only help each other out to a certain limited extent these days. There's all sorts of people watching us, waiting for us to slip up. After that McCabe thing, we get no peace at all."

The little black phone vibrated in McMahon's pocket, indicating that he had received a text message.

* * *

After Palowski had been removed from the Dublin coach he was taken back to Galway Garda station. It didn't take him long to make a lengthy, tearful confession. He was very mixed up and kept confusing the death of his sister with the death of Gerry Maguire. Eventually, Hays and Lyons got a coherent confession from him, enough to bring him to trial in any case and ensure a conviction.

His brother Jakub had travelled to Galway when the news got back to the family. The Palowski parents were in an awful state having virtually lost two of their children in the space of a couple of weeks.

Jakub negotiated the release of Lisa's body, and had it taken back to Poland where she was buried with a full funeral. The nature of her employment in Ireland remained largely undisclosed, and the family turned out in numbers to mourn her passing.

Soon after the burial, her father had a stroke, and died in hospital. Mrs Palowski reckoned that the trauma of the whole thing had been too much for him, and he didn't want to go on living with the dreadful memories of his two children, and the shame that he felt had been brought on the family in any case.

Piotr pleaded guilty at his trial, so very little of the long and complicated story actually got out. The judge was a little sympathetic to the lad. He understood the emotions that had led him to commit his crime, but at the same time had to hand down a stiff sentence as a deterrent to others, and to be seen to be doing the right thing. Piotr served a year in Castlerea jail, and was then transferred to Poland to serve the rest of his sentence in Areszt Prison in Krakow.

Hays heard later from Inspector Kowalski that the lad had been found dead in his cell during the third month of his incarceration there. Kowalski said that they were treating it as suicide, but that he wasn't sure that it really was. Piotr had been given a pretty rough time by his fellow inmates, but it was easier for the authorities to write it off as suicide than to launch a big investigation, and as Kowalski said, "He's dead anyway, no investigation will bring him back to life, so we had best leave it alone."

* * *

You would think that the paint salesman would have learnt a lesson from his encounters with Lisa and the Galway Gardaí, but not a bit of it. After just a few weeks he had sought out another escort girl in Galway and was back in his old routine of visiting her every fortnight when he stayed over in the city.

It went well for a while, but then the girl, who was not as good natured as Lisa had been, began to blackmail him. He had been careless, and one night when he had fallen asleep in her apartment, she found his phone and had copied down the numbers of his work and his home. She had also seen a number of photographs of Gerry, the family man, with his wife and two kids that were stored on the phone.

At first the amounts of money that she asked for were small, so Gerry paid them, not quite knowing how to deal with the situation. But then, as could have been predicted, the girl got greedy, and soon he was being sent demands that he couldn't easily meet.

Eventually, he decided the best course of action was to contact one of the Gardaí that had interviewed him during the business with Lisa. He was put through to Lyons and asked to meet her in a coffee shop in Galway, on the pretext that he had some information that could be useful to the Gardaí.

Lyons went along, but when he told her what his problem was, she was furious. What did he think the Gardaí were for – some sort of counselling service for men who can't keep it in their trousers!

Anyway, she calmed down a bit and took the details of the girl, where she lived, and the address of the web page that she used to attract business.

A few days later, Lyons called on the girl. She was a lovely looking Lithuanian who had come to Ireland thinking she would get work easily, but after a few meaningless jobs as a server in some of the coffee shops in the city, found that it was a much more lucrative business to sell her body, and so she had become an escort like Lisa.

Lyons made it clear to her that she had crossed the line when she had extended her enterprise into blackmail. She was told in no uncertain terms to leave the country without delay, otherwise she would be arrested for soliciting and locked up or deported.

Gerry Byrne continued to play happy families, and no doubt continued with his philandering as well. The detective wondered how long it would be before he got himself into real bother. She had no doubt that their paths would cross again at some stage.

* * *

Ciara continued to drive out to Clifden through the rest of the winter months to see her mother. It was a hard winter, but the woman survived it well, and when the weather improved in spring, she became more agile. The new curtains looked really well in the spare bedroom. Ciara didn't drive along the old bog road anymore. She had been very shaken up by the discovery of a dead body on that awful October night, and didn't want to be reminded of it. Ciara continued to work at About the House, and was soon made up to full manager.

* * *

Mary was the one who came off worst of all out of the double murder. After her husband had been buried, she went back to the cottage on the bog, but couldn't settle there. The tourist office in Clifden had closed for the winter, and she was at a loose end all day with nothing to do but contemplate her situation.

Gerry owned the cottage outright. He had inherited it from his parents a few years before he met Mary, and had spent time doing it up, but she was very uneasy living there with the memories that it held. Gerry of course, believing himself to be invincible, had no life insurance, so not only was Mary left without her man, the father of her two children, but she had no visible means of support either, and no nest egg to fall back on.

In early December that year, she decided to move back to her parents' house in Galway, and lock up the cottage with a view to putting it on the market the following spring when the weather had improved. She gave the hens to a neighbour, and made the place as tidy as she could before leaving it behind, along with the memories of the times she had spent there with Gerry, some of which were very happy ones. Her father couldn't keep his counsel, and chastised her for marrying Gerry in the first place saying, "I told you he was no good, but of course you didn't listen to me. I knew it would all end in tears."

The winter that year was harsh, with several very strong Atlantic storms blowing in from the west. The first bad one had torn five or six slates off the roof of the cottage, and then the rain had got in. With damage to the roof, it wasn't long before the back door of the property blew off its hinges, and after that the house began to disintegrate with remarkable speed.

Mary went to a solicitor in Clifden to arrange the sale of the property the following March. After a bit of research, it transpired that the title to the property had never been transferred from Gerry's parents to him, and there was no title at all to the little dirt track leading down to the house. With the house in a poor state of repair, and with the legal complications, it was virtually unsaleable.

By this time Mary had got a job in a tech firm out in Ballybrit, and her mother was looking after the two kids during the day. She was popular in her new job and had several offers from the men folk to go out on dates, to dinner or to parties, but turned them all down. She was heartily sick of men by now and the damage they could do, so she remained a rather sad widow, focused on her job and the rearing of her two kids. She didn't visit the old bog road ever again.

List of Characters

Detective Inspector Mick Hays – the senior officer in the Galway Detective Unit with many years' experience in crime detection. A confirmed bachelor, Hays is building a strong team in anticipation of an expansion of the unit in the near future.

Detective Sergeant Maureen Lyons – Hays's 'bagman' in Galway, Maureen is constantly trying to prove herself while wrestling with loneliness in her private life. A feisty, ambitious and tough woman with powerful instincts who has a knack of being in the right place at the right time.

Detective Garda Eamon Flynn – known for his tenacity, Flynn wanted to work as a detective since he was a small boy. He develops his skill while working on the case and proves invaluable handling some tricky customers.

Garda John O'Connor – the nerdy and modest junior member of the team is a technical wizard. He loves working with PCs, mobile phones, cameras and anything electronic.

Sergeant Séan Mulholland – happy to take it easy in the quiet backwater of Clifden, Mulholland could have retired by now, but enjoys the status that the job affords him. Not to be hurried, he runs the Garda Station at a gentle pace.

Garda Jim Dolan – works alongside Mulholland and has little ambition to do anything else.

Ciara O'Sullivan – a confident girl from an upper-class Galway family, Ciara has a degree in Retail Management.

Lisa Palowski – a Polish student studying in University College Galway. Lisa has found a way to make extra money in the city, much to the dismay of her family back home.

James McMahon – an arrogant, svelte man-about-town who is not shy about using his influence to stay out of trouble.

Gerry Maguire – a handyman who is a bit too handy when it comes to women. His cool and friendly exterior belies an evil temper and a cruel streak.

Mary Maguire – married Gerry years ago when he swept her off her feet as a teenager. Mary is struggling with her situation, her marriage and the remote place where she now lives.

Gerry Byrne – a philandering paint salesman who travels the country for work but manages to fit in a good few leisure activities as well.

Superintendent Finbarr Plunkett – a wily old character who is politically savvy, he manages the detective unit with subtlety. He's well connected in Galway and exploits his connections to good effect.

Piotr Palowski – Lisa's brother who lives in Poland. Piotr is an emotional person who believes in family values, and is protective of his younger sibling, to a point.

Inspector Kowalski – a tough Polish policeman who cut his teeth during the communist era in Poland and isn't beyond using some of the old techniques to solve crimes.

Inspector Nowak – an ex special forces Pole who can't forget how easy it was to extract confessions years ago before Poland joined the EU.

Sally Fahy – a shy civilian worker attached to the Gardaí in Galway, Sally is careful not to cross the line, but enjoys police work all the same.

If you enjoyed this book, please let others know by leaving a quick review on Amazon. Also, if you spot anything untoward in the paperback, get in touch. We strive for the best quality and appreciate reader feedback.

editor@thebookfolks.com

www.thebookfolks.com

READ THE NEXT BOOK IN THE SERIES:

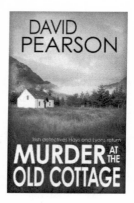

When a nurse finds a reclusive old man dead in his armchair in his cottage, the local Garda surmise he was the victim of a burglary gone wrong. However, having suffered a violent death and there being no apparent robbery, Irish detectives are not so sure. It will take all their wits and training to track down the killer.

SOME OTHER TITLES IN THE SERIES:

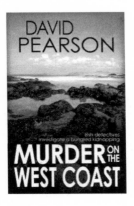

When the Irish police arrive at a road accident, they find evidence of a kidnapping and a murder. Detective Maureen Lyons is in charge of the case but, struggling with self-doubt, when a suspect slips through her fingers she must act fast to save her reputation and crack the case.

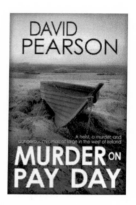

DAVID
PEARSON

A heist, a murder and
dangerous criminals at large in the west of Ireland

MURDER ON
PAY DAY

Following a tip-off, Irish police lie in wait for
a robbery. But the criminals cleverly evade
their grasp. Meanwhile, a body is found
beneath a cliff. DCI Mick Hays' chances of
promotion will be blown unless he sorts out
the mess.

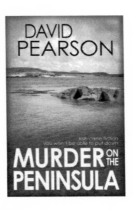

When a body is found on a remote Irish
beach, detectives suspect foul play. Their
investigation leads them to believe the death is
connected to corruption in local government.
But rather than have to hunt down the killer,
he approaches them. With one idea in mind:
revenge.

Made in the USA
Middletown, DE
09 July 2021